STELLAR
ASSIGNMENT

STELLAR ASSIGNMENT

E.C. TUBB

WILDSIDE PRESS

CHAPTER 1

From beneath the pillow the mellifluous voice said, "Wake up! Wake up! It's a wonderful day! The sun is shining, the birds are singing, the wind rustles the leaves of the trees!"

Kevin Blake grunted and kept his eyes firmly closed.

"Wake up!" said the voice urgently. "You are full of vim, vigour and vitality! The blood is rushing through your veins! Today is a new beginning, a time of great opportunity, a period of tremendous promise! Wake up! Wake up!"

"Go to hell," said Kevin thickly.

"Get up!" snapped the voice imperiously. "Rise and shine! It's later than you think! Get up and get going! Wake!"

A pause of five seconds and a harsh, grating noise replaced the feminine tones. Ten seconds later it stopped and he felt a warm glow of satisfaction at having beaten the device. Just as he was sinking back into blissful oblivion a thousand red hot needles jabbed at his naked skin and he reared, yelling from the shock, slamming his hand at the pillow.

"You cow!" he stormed. "You vicious, sadistic, unfeeling bitch! I could have been ill, dying, but what would it matter to you?"

Nothing, of course, nothing at all. It was just a machine and, he thought, sitting on the edge of the bed, a lying one at that. There were no birds, no trees and if the sun was shining it was a safe bet that he wouldn't be able to see it through the usual smog. And he wasn't full of vim, vigour and vitality. He felt worn out, tired, beaten before the day had even started.

Wearily he padded to the shower, wondering at his fatigue. True he had worked late the previous evening but five hours should have been enough and, at his age, loss of sleep shouldn't have dragged him down so low.

It's worry, he decided as he smeared depilatory cream over cheeks and chin. The concern over the new book, the need to start another, the constant doubt as to whether he was writing the right stuff in the right way. And yet what else could he do? Television was out, lacking a union card he didn't stand a chance even if he could produce the crap they demanded. Sex stories were a drug on the market and sadism didn't pay for the paper to write them. To get a novel published meant that you had either to be an attractive woman with an intimate relationship with a publisher or a gigolo making up to his wife. Influence, he thought sourly, washing off the cream and dissolved stubble. Without it you get nowhere.

Teeth brushed, fingernails scrubbed, he left the bathroom and dressed in sober garments; maroon slacks, a scarlet cummerbund, yellow shoes and blouse topped with a maroon bolero. There was no coffee, no tea, no cocoa or yerba mate, not even enough powdered milk to flavour the hot water. Cursing he rose from the store-cupboard. Last night he'd come in late and flopped straight into bed but Duncan should have replaced the essentials. The nurd had probably been entertaining again, dispensing hospitality with a lavish hand, ignoring the needs of his room-mate.

Fuming Kevin strode from the room, slamming the door and heading down the passage towards the elevators. As usual there was a crowd waiting and he only managed to fight his way into the third cage. Fifty stories down and he emerged numb from the pressure into the concourse and headed for a cafeteria. He was lucky, it only took fifteen minutes in line before he collected his coffee and sinker. His luck held and he managed to get a seat. A pimple-faced girl simpered at the pressure of his thigh as he squeezed beside her and a man grunted as his elbow dug into his waist.

"Watch it, buster!"

"Slow down," snapped Kevin. "You want all the room?"

"Just my share," said the man. "I've a right to that, haven't I?"

Kevin dunked his doughnut, not answering and the man gulped the last of his coffee.

"Some people," said the girl as he left. "No consideration for others at all." She moved a little closer, maintaining the contact between hip and knee. "You often eat here?"

"No."

"Nor me. I think eating at home is so much better, don't you? I'm on the sixtieth floor, room 601152, Sylvia Wharton. Another thirty minutes and I can go home. You?"

"Kevin Blake. 502046. I'm just leaving."

"Kevin Blake? The author?" Her expression grew rapturous. "Did you write the Morals Of Mediaeval Man?"

"Yes," said Kevin. "Did you like it?"

"I thought it wonderful!" she gushed, her face glowing. "So full of interesting little details about well, you know. Did they really have to wear chastity belts in those days? And did they have to sleep all together in halls and places? You must be a very clever person to have known all those intimate details."

"Well," said Kevin modestly. "I had to do quite a bit of research."

"And The Sinful Seventies," she continued. "I read it twice because it was so interesting. All that wife-swapping and the drugs and parties and things! I'm so pleased to have met you. Wait until I tell Lorna, that's my sharer, about it. She'll be green with envy. And I must get your other books. What is the latest?"

"Survival in Society," said Kevin quickly. He had obviously misjudged the girl, instead of a pimple-faced nonentity she had charm and grace and a delicate cultural understanding. "I'll autograph it for you if you buy a copy."

"I must get it," she burbled. "I'll put in a request as soon as I get home. I'll call the library right away."

"The library?"

"Of course," she said innocently. "I never buy books, I mean, not actually pay for them. That would be silly, wouldn't it? After all, that's what libraries are for, aren't they?"

Kevin swallowed the last of his coffee and reminded himself that first impressions were usually the correct ones. The girl wasn't cultured and charming at all. She was just a pimple-faced nuisance.

Firmly he rose. "It was nice to have met you," he said. "Don't forget to ask for that book."

"I won't," she promised. "And you won't forget my number, will you? 601152. Sylvia Wharton."

"The book," he insisted, before turning away. "Don't forget it."

After all, every little helped.

* * * *

There was trouble on the subtrans and Kevin was thirty minutes late arriving for work. The checker, a stooped, middle-aged man with a perpetual frown and a lipless mouth stood by the clock, holding out his hand before Kevin could punch his card.

"You're late, Blake," he snapped. "You know the rules. More than two minutes late and you have to report to me. More than ten and you lose an hour. Over that and you have to ask permission to work the shift at all."

"I'm sorry," said Kevin. "I was going to report to you after I hit the clock."

"You're lying," said the checker. "You were going to clock in and go straight to your desk. The floor overseer would think you'd reported to me and I'd allowed you in. It's the last day of the week and the cards would go straight up to the pay office and, if I hadn't been smarter than you figured I wouldn't have known you'd been late at all. Right?"

Kevin sighed. "You're right, Mr Edwards, as usual."

Mollified the checker relaxed. "At least you're not arguing about it. The trouble with most of you people is that you forget I know all the tricks. You don't hold down a job like mine for thirty-five years without staying one jump ahead. The Transworld Trading Company doesn't hire a fool to hold down a position like mine. Excuse?"

"The subtrans broke down. Someone jumped on the track, I think, there was a forty-three minute delay."

"Proof?" Edwards held out his hand. "The conductor would have given you a slip had you asked."

"Sure," agreed Kevin. "Me and all the rest of the passengers. It would have held me up the best part of an hour. But you know that," he added. "And you can check that I'm telling the truth. If you find I'm lying I'll lose a day's pay."

Edwards sucked in his cheeks. "Well—" he began, then changed his mind. "All right, Blake, you've a good record so I'll pass you in this time. See me after, eh? I reckon it's worth an hour, don't you?"

"Sure, Mr Edwards. And thanks."

Savagely Kevin punched his card and handed it to the checker. He could argue but then the nurd would stand on his authority and he would lose the shift. If he neglected to pay he would have the checker riding on his neck. If he complained he would get exactly nowhere. After thirty-five years with the firm Edwards had friends in the right places.

Hepton looked up from his work as he passed his desk. Like Kevin he was a clerk, unlike him he was old, withered, hanging on to his job with a vicious desperation. He threw over a sheaf of bills.

"Top-office wants this checked in double-quick time. As you weren't in I volunteered to take care of it. I told the overseer I figured you were sick."

"That was nice of you," said Kevin bitterly.

"Well, you know how it is. I like to help out when I can."

"By making certain he knew I wasn't in. Hell, with friends like you I don't need enemies."

"I was only trying to help."

"I know what you were trying to do," said Kevin. "Why didn't you just keep that big mouth of yours shut instead?"

Glowering he studied the bills. A consignment catfur mittens had been lost in transit to the colony on Tejat III. Another of diamond-tipped drills had never reached Ahmand of the Sirian system even though they had been paid for in advance. The Government of the Proxima Centauri Federation was annoyed at having received fifty tons of spangled cod-pieces instead of the cans of processed dog meat they had expected. The Ku Wang consortium of Achernar V could not understand why they had been sent a cargo of synthetic gills when they had most clearly ordered one of collapsible blow-pipes together with poisoned darts for same.

A routine day's work, thought Kevin sourly, something which any one of the five hundred clerks could have handled, but Hepton had had to make himself look take the opportunity of making his colleague look small. Sickness was frowned on by the Transworld Company. It would mean a black mark on his record.

Tiredly he began to stab buttons on his desk, checking consignments with the main computer, cross-checking, tracking down. The catfur mittens had been shipped by mistake to Sleeth. The drills were still in the warehouse waiting final clearance. The cod-pieces had been mislabelled and he arranged for the transfer of cargoes. The synthetic gills were a problem and it took him an hour to discover they should have been sent to Aquarion where, no doubt, the fish-folk were wondering how to use the blowpipes. Another arrangement to transfer cargoes and the thing was done.

Yawning Kevin assembled the papers, marked each with a note of the action taken and dropped the sheaf into the appropriate chute. Before he could reach for another stack from the pile accumulated on his desk the girl came round with the mid-shift coffee. She was a nice, well-built girl and he leaned back watching the play of her hips as she moved with her trolley between the desks.

"Women!" snapped Hepton spitefully. "That's all you youngsters think about. Why, when I was your age I had to keep my nose to the grindstone. No time for day-dreaming then. It was work, work, work all the time."

"Sure," said Kevin. "And what has it got you?"

"A job. A pension in another ten years. Security."

"Hell," said Kevin.

"That's what you think." Hepton was defensive. "Let me tell you there are a lot worse things than having a steady job. You ever seen the dormitories? The jobless on the streets? The beggars? You don't remember the riots like I do and you're lucky. They were bad. So were the hunger years. I bet you've never had to share a room with five others. A small room at that."

"I share," said Kevin.

"Sure you do. We all do. But you share with one or two at the most."

"One," said Kevin.

"Twelve-hour turnabout," said Hepton. "You call that sharing? I'll bet there are days when you don't even see each other. I remember when you had to wait for a man to get up so you could use the bed. Things were bad before they threw up the towers."

"Knock it off," said Kevin. "I've heard it all before."

"Youngsters," said Hepton. He gulped at his coffee and set aside the empty cup. "You don't know when you're well off."

No, thought Kevin, finishing his coffee, that's true enough. We've never known when we were well off. To some of the ancients this world would seem a paradise, warmth, food, clothing, non-physical work, entertainment, decent medical attention. The future has always looked glamorous to the past. But we have to pay for it. No birds, no trees, no sunshine which we can enjoy. Not the majority of us, that is. The rich, yes, they've always had it good, but not the rest. From one box to another, he thought, looking around. That's what life has become. Moles crawling around in a concrete maze. Two-legged ants in a man-made mountain.

Well, to hell with it. Work was just something to get through. Another three hours and he could start to live again.

* * * *

Julia Frost was forty-two years old, an unconfirmed spinster, a secret romantic and a natural-born librarian. She displayed expensive teeth as Kevin approached, set down the pile of books she carried and hastily dusted herself down. The simple, red, yellow and black striped dress she wore did nothing for her figure but managed to hide the supporting garments she wore beneath. Her face was a sallow brown, her hair a darker brown fastened in a bun, her eyes were a matching colour. A mole to one side of her mouth sported three lank hairs.

"Kevin!" she greeted. "I was beginning to think you'd forgotten us." The plural was for herself and the books. "I expect you've been busy, is that it? All those parties to launch the new book, the publishers, all those women. Yes?"

"No."

"No parties?"

"No parties. No publishers fighting for the rights to my next work. No women." He sighed. "It's not going well, Julia. If things don't pick up soon I'll have to get a second job."

Immediately she was concerned. "As bad as that? I refuse to believe it. It's a good book, Kevin. A fine book. Once the right people read it, it will make your name. "You'll be famous."

"We'll both be famous, Julia." He dropped his hand on her shoulder, squeezed. "I won't forget all the help you've given me. If I ever get rich you'll be my personal secretary and then we'll collaborate as I promised. But, in the meantime, well, we'll just have to keep hoping."

"And working," she reminded. "I've been going through the stacks and I've dug up quite a lot of useful items. What will the next one be about, Kevin? Sex? Warfare? The interplay of human relationships? The new morality? Expanding horizons?"

She was a gem, a jewel, a veritable gold mine and he couldn't do without her. Not just for her encouragement but for her specialised knowledge and for her access to the mountain of books within the library. Too many books, he thought bitterly. Two hundred years of continuous output not counting those before the middle of the nineteenth century. Until the twentieth the production hadn't been too bad but then had come the flood, the deluge, the superabundance of reading matter. Millions of books churned from the presses, an uncountable stack of paperbacks, entire forests converted into material to bear the printed word.

No wonder publishers weren't interested in new material, he mused as he followed Julia into the depths of the library. With such a backlog to draw on why should they worry about things like royalties and cultivating new writers? All they had to do was to reissue the old titles, the best-sellers of a century ago, souped up a little maybe, brought up to date, but basically the old material. There was material enough to bring out a dozen titles a day for the foreseeable future, repeating for every new generation of readers. A worm, he thought, feeding on its own tail but growing so that the tail never became exhausted. A continual feed-back cycle which effectively made it both unnecessary and uneconomical to seek new authors. He was lucky to have sold what he had.

"How about religion?" she asked brightly, halting before a desk piled high with volumes. "I've sorted out a dozen works on the subject. Perhaps, if you studied them?"

"I must think about it," he said hastily. "I need to get the feel."

"Perversions?" Julia was determined to be helpful and she was in no hurry to leave. He looked so tired, she thought, so worried. She longed to wrap her arms around him and cradle his head on her bosom. To run her fingers through his hair and soothe away his cares. He's so young, she told herself, so vulnerable. "Sex seems

to be a good subject," she urged. "Flagellations, fetish-objects, fel-
latio. Of course," she hinted, "you'd have to do quite a bit of research."

With her? Kevin shuddered at the thought. Not for the first time
he had the impression that he was a fly trapped in a spider's web. He
could walk away, of course, but if he did he would lose too much.

"Not sex," he said firmly. "At least, not that kind. How about
drugs? Wasn't there something about men trying to find the ulti-
mate by the use of hallucinogens?"

"Which period? The seventies had quite a lot about it and there
was revived interest about thirty years ago when the MacMillian
Amendment removed the restrictions on sale and supply."

He brooded for a moment. Thirty years ago was a little too
close. Authors could still be alive and there could be trouble with
copyrights, also some readers had long memories. Better make it
the seventies. Eighty years was long enough and there was no point
in taking unnecessary chances.

"I'll start digging them out," she promised when he gave his
decision. "In the meantime there's quite a bit of relevant matter in
those I've already selected. Now be a good boy and get down to
your research. Would you like some coffee?"

"No thanks."

"Tea? Yerba mate?"

"Later," he said. "In a couple of hours. I want to get down to it."

She smiled approval as she left and reluctantly he dug into the
heaped piles. This was the part he hated, the questing and prying,
the selecting, the accumulation of basic material. A page here, a
chapter there, a paragraph from somewhere else. Skipping, dipping,
a vulture pecking at meaty bones. A ghoul, he thought dispassion-
ately, stealing from the dead, living on the product of other men's
brains. At times he didn't even have to change a word, just assemble
the accumulated material to form a coherent whole. Mostly it was a
matter of reduction, cutting down the inflated verbosity, condensing
and lightening with an eliminating pencil.

A copier stood beside the desk and he settled down to work, the
stack of duplicated pages mounting at his side. The effect of hal-
lucinogenic drugs on the sexual impulse, he decided. A useless title

but it gave him a work-guide. Plenty of case histories and personal confessions which would easily allow plenty of spice as well as taking up a lot of space. Perversions too, Julia had a point there, and they would be simple to introduce. Freud would be the man for that. His peculiar Victorianism would have to be remodelled but his patients had certainly used their imaginations.

"How are we getting on?" Julia had returned, a steaming cup in her hand. Casually she examined the top sheet on the pile. "Kevin! Are you sure this will do? It seems awfully heavy to me."

"It won't be in the final draft," he promised. The cup held genuine Indian tea and he enjoyed the fragrance before sipping the brew. "Anyway, this is just basic research and I'll probably discard most of it when you find more appropriate sources."

"Of course," she watched him for a moment, eyes bright in the reflected light of the desk lamp. "Don't work too hard now."

"I won't."

"Maybe you should rest for a while. I've a cot in the office which you could use if you wanted."

"I'd better not," he said, wondering how long he would be alone should he yield to the suggestion. Not long from the look of her. "I've got to get on with the new book. And it must be near your end of shift. You don't want me around when your relief comes."

"It wouldn't matter," she hinted. "Sally is broad minded."

"You're the Head Librarian," he reminded. "You have to keep up appearances. I wouldn't like to do anything to cause you trouble."

His concern touched her, the dear boy was always so considerate, sometimes too considerate. But artists were like that. They tended to live in a world of their own and the research must take all of his energies. He nodded when she mentioned it.

"It's something I have to put up with," he admitted. "There's no other way. But honestly, Julia, I don't know what I'd do without you."

Which was true enough, he thought as she left him to get on with it. But in many ways he was becoming quite an accomplished liar.

CHAPTER 2

It was late when he left the library and what could be seen of the sky was a dull, angry pink from reflected lights, smog and cloud. Above the mess was clean air, the moon and stars and he realised that he had never seen them, not really, only as glittering dots on a television screen. Captain Cosmos, he thought sourly. Sergeant Starflight. Galactic General and the stomach churning Pirates of Pegasus, programmes in which stalwart heroes rescued nubile maidens from slavering monsters with tireless monotony. Writers, he mused. People who turned out stuff like that should be shot. And yet was he any better? Did the pap he plagiarised have any real, greater merit? Beneath the superficial veneer of educated gloss wasn't he pandering to jaded appetites just as the television writers were?

Grimly he hefted the bundle of copied pages under his arm. This was no time to get philosophical and to doubt the value of what he did. The stuff had to be whipped into shape, edited, set in order and then neatly typed on virgin paper. With any sort of luck at all *Drug Debauchery* might actually ring the bell.

Duncan was home when he arrived. He lay sprawled on the bed, a tall, thin, ungainly figure in polka dot slacks and blouse. He was older than Kevin with a face seamed with cynical lines and eyes which always seemed slightly bloodshot. As a debt collector he worked at night and should have been working now. Pointedly Kevin glanced at his watch.

Duncan saw the gesture and shrugged. "So I'm an hour after time," he admitted. "But I've got a shift off, I'm flat broke and my girl has let me down. Could you lend me a little?"

"No."

"You got paid today."

"I got paid," Kevin agreed. "But I've got debts and expenses." He dumped the pile of paper on the table. "And I've got to work," he added. "I don't want to be hard about this but we have an agreement."

"The place is all yours until 9.00 tomorrow," said Duncan. He reared up and sat on the edge of the bed. "I know it but I won't be any trouble. You have the bed and I'll use the floor. Hell, man, you wouldn't want me to wander all night, would you?"

"No," said Kevin. Territorial rights firmly established he could afford to be generous. "Did you get some coffee?"

"With what? I told you, I'm flat broke."

"Then it's lucky that I did." Kevin produced a tin of synthetic Brazilian from a pocket. "How about making yourself useful?"

From above the rush of water in the miniscule kitchen Duncan yelled; "Something I forgot to tell you. Your agent called. I said you'd ring him back."

"Ransom? You sure?"

"Round face, small beard, almost bald a scar over one eye and hairs growing from his ears."

"That's Ransom. What did he want?"

"He didn't tell me. Call him and find out."

Digging coins from his pocket Kevin paid the machine and punched the number. Ransom beamed at him from screen. "Kevin, my boy! You're looking well! Everything going well?"

"You tell me," said Kevin. "Made any more sales yet?"

"I'm trying, boy! I'm trying all the time! You know me, how I operate, never give the customers a chance to relax. I'm chasing them all the time. But it isn't easy, boy. It's a long way from that. To be truthful it's damned hard. But I keep plugging, boy, you can be sure of that."

"Good. Why did you call?"

"A break! A great opportunity! A fish I've been hoping to catch for a long time." Ransom radiated enthusiasm. "You've heard of Felicita Marmot? A big wheel on the upper deck. A patroness of the arts, society charity organiser, backs select exhibitions and has influence where it counts. She read your book and wants to meet you. Take down the address," he rattled it off as Kevin searched for a stylo. "Be there at midnight. And, boy, be ready to sell yourself. This could be the opening we've been waiting for. Contacts, interest the right people, but if any of them try to corner you refer them to me. Right?"

"Wait a minute," snapped Kevin. "Which book did she read?"

"The latest, of course. Survival In Society. It's up to you now, boy. I've got you the chance so make the most of it."

Kevin frowned as he turned from the dead screen. Duncan, coffee cup in hand, nodded towards the instrument.

"I heard. You're going, of course."

"I suppose I'll have to. It'll be a waste of time though. I've been to these parties before. All they want is a freak to yak at."

"So what?" Duncan was cynical. "You'll get free food and drinks. And it could be more than that. I've heard of Felicita Marmot. She fancies herself as an artist and has plenty of the right kind of backing. Money," he explained. "She's loaded. You could be on a good thing here, Kevin, if you play it right."

"I'll go," said Kevin. "I'll stand around and make the right noises and be polite. It won't do any good but I'll go."

"Not like that, you won't." Duncan was firm. "Not with those clothes and that attitude."

"What's wrong with them?"

"They belong to a nice-mannered little clerk, that's what. Hell, man, she doesn't want that. She wants a real, tough, hairy character and that's what you've got to be." Duncan looked at him with a critical eye. "You've got advantages," he said. "You're tall and good-looking and you've got plenty of bulk. How old are you? Twenty-six? Knock off a few, tell her you're twenty-one and if she probes feed her a line. Feed it to her anyway. Lie your head off and make an impression. What was the title of that book? Survive in Society? Well, now's your chance to prove the value of what you wrote. You're going to survive."

"Act, you mean," said Kevin. Dubiously he shook his head. "I don't know. I don't like it. Why the hell can't they take me as I am?"

Duncan was brutal. "Because you're nothing, that's why. A part of the background. Put you in a crowd and you'd be invisible."

Kevin glowered, feeling the sting of savage truth, but Duncan was right. He'd done nothing to be proud of. Even his writing was a pathetic attempt to gain individuality and his routine job was deserving only of contempt. But, damn it, he could learn.

"The clothes first," said Duncan, forging ahead, gaining pleasure from his mastery. "I've some old gear you can wear and we'll rough it up a little. Now the way to act. Don't just stand around saying nothing. Stay away from the booze and watch your tongue. Be arrogant, rude if they try to put you down, smoulder if you can manage it. Don't vanish into the background. Grab a good-looking girl and proposition her. You'll be up against tough competition and you don't want to be swamped. And always remember that everyone at the party is a phoney. And lie, man, lie all the time. Hell," he snapped impatiently as Kevin shook his head. "You're a writer, aren't you? You deal with words. Lying's your profession. It should be easy."

Kevin took a deep breath. "Why not?" he surrendered. "What have I got to lose?"

* * * *

Felicita Marmot's apartment was a penthouse topping a block in the fashionable quarter and Kevin arrived an hour late. Duncan had advised it as he had also advised the inward application of five ounces of neat alcohol. Now, fortified with Dutch courage, determined to play the whole thing like a game, Kevin rammed his thumb against the doorbell.

"Blake," he snapped at the impeccably dressed steward who opened the door. "I'm invited. Tell the hostess I'm here."

He moved forward before the man could object and stood staring at the scene. The room was vast, adorned with framed objects, carpeted, dimly lit and seemed to be filled with a host of people in fancy dress. Beads, buckskins, bangles and beards stood, talked or danced all around. A wide table to one side held an assortment of food and drink. Music came from a group sitting cross-legged and twanging strings. More came from a bunch playing flutes and hitting drums. The mingled odours of perfume and incense caught at his nostrils.

"Mr Blake?" Felicita came towards him. She was a young fifty, superbly dressed, beautiful in an artificially cosmetised way. Precious stones glittered on the hand and wrist she extended. "Mr Kevin Blake? Author of Survival in Society?"

"Among other things, yes." He took the hand and pressed it, letting her see the chunky ring Duncan had slipped on his little finger. As a ring it made a fine knuckleduster. "It is a pleasure to meet you."

"It was good of you to come," she responded. "I'd almost given you up. You haven't been to one of my little gatherings before, have you Mr Blake?"

"Kevin," he said. "A title means a label and labels mean pigeonholes. I hate things to be compartmented."

"Well, Kevin," she said. "As I was saying, I do like people to be on time."

"Time?" He glowered, a free soul rebelling at the chafing restrictions of a mundane world. "Felicita, you surprise me. An artist such as yourself to talk of such a meaningless concept. What is time? In an hour we can live a lifetime. In a decade we could but experience a minute of personal existence. It is all in the mind. In my next work I intend to prove that duel-comprehension of temporal flow is not only instinctive but essential if we are ever to grasp the reality lying beyond the scope of our limited senses. You follow me, of course?"

"Yes," she said, "Naturally. As a student of the Vegas I too have made certain discoveries. We must discuss them sometimes."

"The Vegas," he said. "Hindu mythology. It is a tragedy that so much of the Greater Truth has been lost to the general population. Not," he added, "that the secret writings contain more than a hint of the True Path, but the signs are there for those with the correct vision to see. In my book, Rites of Religion, I delved into the matter in some depth. Did you agree with my conclusions?"

Without hesitation she said; "Of course. It was a most fascinating work."

Cruelly, as he hadn't yet written the book, he said, "And chapter seventeen, did you find that of interest?"

"All your books contain a mine of information," she assured. "But I mustn't be selfish and keep you all to myself. Do come and meet some of the others."

He met a man naked to the waist bearing a tattooed crucifix on his chest who claimed to be in direct communication with Saint Peter. Another who had created a new art form by using knotted string. A girl who spoke to ants. A woman who had been seduced by a demon. A dozen assorted artists and a man who wore stripes of black, brown, yellow and white paint over his face.

"I am the Universal Man," he said as Felicita moved away after the introduction. "On me all colours are as one, all races joined in true harmony. I am a symbol of the existing world, a child of Mother Earth."

"A false symbol," said Kevin shortly. "A stinking racist."

"You call me that!"

"On your skin you have painted a territorial region," continued Kevin, not bothering to lower his voice. "Does the universe consist of Man alone? Where is the fur, the feathers, the scales and wings, the gills and tendrils? Are you so blind that you cannot lift your eyes from the dirt beneath your feet? Is your comprehension so limited that you refuse to recognise that we all, from the smallest thing which crawls to the titans which use planets for stepping stones, are a part of the single gestalt of universal intelligence?"

A girl standing to one side said; "You don't have to be so insulting."

She seemed normal enough, he decided, looking at her. Tall and well-shaped with loose hair and naked limbs. She wore a chiton of green and gold, heavy earrings and a medallion of Nefertiti hanging from a golden chain. She looked a little startled as he stepped close and rested his hands on her hips.

"You are beautiful," he said. "Let us dance."

"I don't—"

"You will," he insisted, urging her towards the centre of the floor. "You must."

They danced. Her name was Claudia and she was a student of social sciences and primitive religions. "Do you know," she said as they moved slowly over the floor, "that on Cantara the males of the Kleegha tribe are not allowed to see a woman until they reach puberty? They are kept in isolation until it is time for mating. Then, after cohabitation, they are sent away again until the offspring is born. Can you imagine the result?"

"Too well," he murmured into her hair. "How does the custom affect the economic development of the region?"

She told him, volunteered more items of similar information, then squealed as he abruptly lifted her from the floor. "What are you doing?"

"Checking your weight." Gently he set her down. "I tend to be old fashioned in certain things. I like to be sure of carrying my wives over the threshold."

"You're married?"

"Not now."

"Before?"

"Three times," he lied. "It was the only way I could get a roof. Do you have money?"

"My parents have. Would it make a difference?"

"No," he said, and almost meant it. "Not if you don't object to doing without. Let me know what you decide."

"I'll do that," she promised, then looked over his shoulder. "I think Felicita wants you. She keeps staring at us."

Business, thought Kevin as, leaving Claudia, he moved towards where she stood. A middle-aged man stood at her side, hair greying at the temples, mouth a firm gash over his jaw. He wore conservative clothing and seemed as out of place in this gathering as a pigeon among parrots. A scatter of others, younger, dressed for the occasion, stood behind and around. Executive types, decided Kevin, studying them. Junior administrators having a little fun. Parasites on Felicita's wealth and catering to her whims. As phoney as the rest but in a more subtle, more acceptable way. The promotors of exhibitions, art dealers, commercial writers, the cream riding the top of the artistic crowd.

Now, if ever, was the time to sell himself.

"Kevin!" she greeted him with a smile. "I'm so glad you could tear yourself away from that charming little creature. I'd like you to meet Paul Tarvainen. Paul, this is Kevin Blake."

"Blake," said the middle-aged man. "Did you write Survival In Society?"

"Among other things, yes."

"I'm not interested in the other things. Is the book your own work?"

Kevin felt a prickle of caution. "What are you getting at?"

"I'm not getting at anything. I asked a straight question and I want a straight answer. Did you write the book?"

"Of course I wrote it," snapped Kevin. Attack was the best form of defence. "What the hell do you think I did? Steal it?"

"It reminds me of something I read as a boy," said Tarvainen. "My father had a copy in his library. It's a long time ago now and I've forgotten details, but there seemed to be a similarity. Your premise that men are really animals living in a concrete jungle. That emotions can be induced or dissipated by the correct stance and expression, things like that. It's odd."

Damn it, but the man was close! With an inward effort Kevin maintained his composure. "Certain things are basic to the human race," he said coldly. "We eat, feel, think and react. We know fear and we know anger. We are concerned with territorial rights and possessions. It could be that the subject has been touched on before, I'd be surprised if it hadn't, but that has nothing to do with me. My work is original."

Tarvainen grunted. "Keep your shirt on. I just wanted to know."

"And you've found out." Kevin relaxed, smiling, now was the time to salve the man's pride. "I've just given you an example. By doubting my integrity you encroached on my territorial rights in the sense that you tended to diminish my importance. How else could I have reacted other than with aggression?"

"You could have backed down," said Tarvainer. "By withdrawal you could have dissipated my anger."

"And allowed you possession of the field," agreed Kevin. "That's true, but you weren't displaying anger, only determination and yet the threat was still present. Had I backed you would have been convinced that your implied accusation that I had committed plagiarism was true. Anger would have been the inevitable result. My withdrawal then would have appeared an admission of guilt." He smiled. "Well, one thing is clear, you have certainly read the book."

"I've studied it," corrected Tarvainen. "If I came at you with a knife what would you do?"

"Study the possibilities. Escape if I could, submit if I had to, fight if there was no alternative. A threat is usually implied or actual," he explained. "A man with a bared knife could be implying that he will use it if you continue to resist his will. It could be a personal aggression-symbol which he needs to bolster his own ego. Or it could be the visible evidence that he intends to destroy his opponent. A correct evaluation of intent enables a man to decide on the appropriate course of action."

Tarvainen was unsatisfied. "You're evading the question," he protested. "Suppose that I was to whip out a knife, now, at this moment, and start moving towards you. What would you do?"

"Nothing," said Kevin flatly.

"Paul!" Felicita was worried. "You're not going to—"

"Of course not," he snapped. "It's an academic question." He glared at Kevin. "What makes you say that?"

"You have no reason to be aggressive towards me and certainly no reason to wish me dead. Also you are a product of our society, physical violence does not come easily to you. And you have shown no sign of being insane. Therefore any such act as you propose can only be a theatrical gesture and I would treat it as such."

"And if I were different?" Tarvainen demanded. "A barbarian, say, what then?"

"Cultural mores would, of course, alter the entire situation," said Kevin glibly, feeling that he was safe on firm ground. "Each society must be taken and evaluated by the conditions prevalent within its own culture. Before I could answer that question I would need far more data than you have given. A barbarian, you say. All right, but what of the circumstances? Not even a barbarian kills just for the sake of it. Always there is a reason. Would I have offended his gods? His hospitality? His concept of correct behaviour? Would he be trying to collect scalps to adorn his costume? Would he have need of reaffirming his masculinity, and why? You see how complex the matter becomes."

"I know how complex it becomes," muttered Tarvainen. "All right, Blake. Thank you. Now I've got things to think about."

Dismissed, Kevin wandered over to the table and pecked at the food. It was good food but he couldn't enjoy it. So much for Duncan's tuition. He'd made his mark, sure, but for what? So that someone could have the chance to apply the thumbscrews and test the reactions of a weirdie. That's what the nurd takes me for, he told himself bitterly. And how can I blame him? Dressed in rubbish, acting the fool, showing off and flexing non-existent muscles. Savagely he glared at the other members of the circus. Fools, the lot of them, prancing idiots too busy scratching each other's backs and maintaining a mutual illusion to realise just how they appeared to normal people. And he had become them.

Well, he thought, what the hell. I'm here now so I might as well make the best of it. What have I got to lose?

The champagne was good but a little too light for his taste. The whisky was better and the brandy better still. A little hock to wash it down and some white rum to follow. Vodka for the novelty and kummel because he hadn't tasted it before. And then back to the food, peaches in brandy, pineapple in kirsch, grapes in campari and apple soaked in calvados. The rich, he thought, did themselves well.

"I like to see a man eating." He turned as Felicita suddenly appeared at his side. "And you are a big man. Those muscles of yours must use a lot of energy." Her slim hand squeezed his bicep. "Did Paul upset you?"

"Is a mountain disturbed by the touch of a breeze?" He blinked, wondering why he had said that, the words had simply popped out of his mouth. The combination of drinks must have oiled his tongue. "No, he didn't upset me. Is he a friend of yours?"

"A business acquaintance. Why do you ask?"

"He had a proprietary air. As if he owned you."

"No man owns me!" she said sharply and then, in a gentler tone of voice; "Paul is very rich and, I'm afraid, the very rich tend to be very arrogant. It isn't wholly their fault, I suppose, so many people are willing to crouch at their feet. You made a refreshing change. I think you impressed him." The hand squeezed again. "You certainly impressed me. Why haven't we met before?"

"All things must have a beginning." He looked beyond her to where little groups of guests sat clustered on the floor. The string band had vanished and some of the people he had seen appeared to be missing. "You are a very unusual woman," he said. "You have the gift of humanity."

"Meaning?"

"You are not as arrogant as your friend."

"Paul?" She shrugged. "Perhaps, but then I'm not as rich. And arrogance can take many forms. Mine is that I consider myself to be a judge of art. What do you think of my collection?" she gestured to the framed objects on the walls. "Come and study them. I would appreciate your opinion as to their merit."

Cautiously he followed her across the room, cursing himself for having drunk so much. This was no time to become inane or slur his words. Fighting the tendency to grin he managed to obtain a sullen look of brooding introspection. Carefully he came to a halt beside his hostess and stared at the wall. A mass of coloured scraps stuck on a board. A three-dimensional depiction of a crushed worm. A tangle of knotted string. An ebon background on which rested three strands of wire, one silver, one gold, the other scarlet. An expanse of thick paint cratered with scattered pits. The other walls bore similar assemblies of junk.

A test? Surely no one in their right mind could value such rubbish. And yet it had been framed with care and placed with obvious dedication. Was some of it the product of her own hands? Most probably, but which? It would help to know.

He moved slowly along the display, concentrating not on the objects but the woman. The alcohol seemed to have clarified his vision so that he caught the slight tension, the unconscious gesture of the hand, and looked at the item before him. It was the black background with the three strands of wire.

Recklessly he gambled. "This," he said slowly. "It has something unique. It catches the eye and holds the attention. The others have their own merit," he added, coppering his bet, "Too much to absorb all in a moment. But this..." He let his voice trail into silence as he stepped closer.

Around him he sensed the gathering of an audience and the challenge helped to stimulate his imagination. Cautiously he watched his hostess, noting her mounting anxiety as he dragged out the minutes, stepping back, forward, back again, his eyes half-closed. Deliberately he sat cross-legged before the object of his study.

"Words," he said. "We each work within the framework of our chosen medium and mine is words. Harsh things, rigid, subject to a discipline of their own. We can expand the boundaries a little, invent new forms, patterns, frames of comprehension, but in the end it all comes down to marks on paper. Regular, marching, chanelling thought. But this! A concept so vast, concentrated in a space so small as to almost defy description. Poetry, caught and held and translated into this narrow field. A mathematical equation is ungainly in comparison. Pure symbolism displayed in stark beauty and, to each, it brings its own message. To me it sings of love and flame and eternal life. It whispered in a second, spoke in a minute, shouted in more. Given time it would thunder with the sound of disrupting stars. If ever a pattern could explain the universe this is it."

He fell silent, brooding, hearing the faint tapping of the drums, the wail of the flute.

Felicita drew in her breath. "You like it," she said. "But what does it mean?"

Had he guessed wrongly? A glance reassured him. The woman looked dazed, unbelieving, yet relaxed.

"Mean? To whom? To me? To you? Can there be any doubt? And yet we are the slave of our senses and barriers fog purity wherever we look. But, like an exploding star, this penetrates the murk of intellectual dust. The background is night, the ebon nothingness which existed before the dawn of creation, the light-absorbing substance which is all around us, within us, dulling the Greater Truth. The sombre half of the ying-yang depiction. Night," he repeated. "Darkness. Space. The fabric of the universe. The nighted womb and the ebon grave. Ignorance and intolerance. Negation and yet, also the canvas on which the master paints the pains and struggles of life. All embracing, all-encompassing. Look at it and it fills the vision with emptiness. Into it you could lose your soul.

"And against it, a shining light of brilliance, the silver strand of hope, of light, of the second half of the ying-yang. A dazzling thing which drives back the dark and yet recognises that it is still there, that it will always be there, waiting, lurking, ready to again fill our vision. That alone would have created a masterpiece but there is more. A shaft of golden effulgence, the very choice of God, the presence of the Divine, the symbol of all mysteries which have ever been and ever will be. Gold and silver matched against the encroaching dark and in such a juxtaposition that there can be no doubt what the message conveys. Hope and light, mystery and enchantment, brightness and Divine grace. And yet there is more! The scarlet thread of life itself! Of blood and fire and agony and pain. The agony of achievement, the pain of birth, the scarlet bloom which must always accompany creation. God and light and humanity set each in their correct order, each given their proper place, each combining, one to the other in perfect balance and harmony.

"Time is too limited," he continued in a sombre tone. "A day studying the deeper complexities of this work would not be long enough to appreciate its subtle qualities. A volume would be too short to set down in the cold words which cramp description of the message it brings. How to describe a universe? How to describe creation? How to set down in restricted symbols the blazing inspiration of genius? It cannot be done."

He fell silent, looking into space, brooding like some Greek hero studying the walls of Troy. A mystic pondering the immutable. A man enraptured by a sudden glimpse of stunning beauty.

CHAPTER 3

Felicita drew a deep breath and said, shakily; "Well! I never thought—Kevin, my dear boy! You are incredible! Such depths of insight! Such a magnificent perception!"

From the gathering a thin man, bearded, dressed as a guru said quickly; "Felicita, my dear, how often have I told you that you underestimate yourself? From the first moment I saw your masterpiece I have been working on a mantra to describe it in a single phrase. The symbols elude me but they will come."

"It has inspired my finest poem," said a girl eager to get in on the act, and immediately began to quote:

> *Genesis growing gathering gloom*
> *Silver shining straightly severe*
> *Gold giving greater grace*
> *Scarlet showing sinful space*

"Our friend has the advantage," interrupted the man who knotted string. "I am, myself, working on a paean composed of fifteen miles of coloured rope which will take an area of two thousand square feet to display to its best advantage."

"I have seen the light!" announced the Universal Man. "Tomorrow I wear nothing but gold, silver, scarlet and black. Your message, Felicita, will be obvious to all with the eyes to see."

"I must tell my friends," whispered the girl who spoke to ants.

Fighting his desire to laugh Kevin rose and took his hostess by the hand. Quietly he said; "I own nothing that you would not throw away, but all I have I will lay at your feet for the privilege of studying your work at greater leisure."

"You silly, boy!" Her hand rose and touched his hair. "Of course you may see it again. Often, I hope. And now let us have a glass of champagne."

By God, I've done it, thought Kevin as he followed her to the buffet. I've registered the fact that I exist if nothing else. The ease of it baffled him. A load of nonsense spouted about a load of rubbish and he had become the centre of attention. Duncan was right, he told himself as the woman picked up two glasses of champagne. These people don't want the truth, they want someone to maintain their illusions.

Taking the proffered glass he lifted it and said; "A toast, Felicita. To your beauty—may it never fade."

Their glasses touched.

"My beauty," she said thoughtfully as she lowered her glass. "Not my art?"

"The two are as one."

"You were really impressed?"

Instinct warned him to be cautious. This woman could not be the total fool she appeared and he must not make himself akin to the rest. He took another sip of the wine and set down the glass.

"I was effusive," he said, "but with reason. Your work reminded me of something I once saw in the jungles of Yucatan. A weathered column of stone wreathed with vines on which some ancient artist had drawn three lines. It was late in the afternoon and the setting sun caught them, filling one with shadow, another with brightness. Their juxtaposition was unusual, deliberately asymmetrical, and I spent an hour watching the interplay of light over the pattern. When I saw your work I understood what that artist had attempted. The objects, in themselves, are meaningless but their relationship to each other, their colours—" He broke off and shook his head. "Emotions," he said. "We need a new language to describe them."

"You've lived hard," she said and her eyes examined his clothing, worn, garish, but clean. "And yet you seem so young."

"My father was a prospector," he invented. "I never knew my mother. We travelled a lot and when he died of fever I had to make my own way."

"Claudia tells me you've had three wives."

"A native girl at fifteen," he hastily improvised. She died in childbirth. An older woman when I was two years older. She was very jealous."

"With reason, I expect. And?"

"A librarian," he said, thinking of Julia. "A year ago. It lasted three months." He picked up her glass and handed it to her. "Let's not talk about me," he urged. "Are you working on anything at this moment?"

To his relief she was and they chatted a while about the various merits of sand, mud, plaster and wet cement as a medium for abstract designs made by dropping balls of ice on the yielding material.

Then, regretfully, she shook her head. "This is most interesting, Kevin, I could talk to you for hours, but I can't ignore my other guests. Do please help yourself to anything you want."

He'd already had too much. His head was buzzing with a trapped swarm of bees and he doubted his ability to maintain his façade. And he was having trouble with his enunciation.

"I must go," he said. "It's been wonderful meeting you, Felicita."

"You'll come again?"

He nodded and walked carefully to the door. Outside he leaned against a wall and stared at his watch, discovering that it was four in the morning. Five hours and he'd have to be on the job. Damn it! Why had he drunk so much?

A passage led from the door, turning as it ran towards the elevator. Grimly he plodded down it feeling that he was racing against time. He had to get home before the full effects rose to hit him. Turning the corner he almost bumped into two men.

They were young, soberly dressed, innocuous-seeming types who were just waiting for something. A girl, perhaps, or maybe they were on their way to the party late as it was. One of them stared at Kevin and nodded to his companion.

"Just a moment." He stepped forward, blocking the passage. "Is your name Blake?"

"That's right." Kevin lurched towards his left, half turning from his questioner. "If you want the party it's straight down there." He straightened, swinging his right hand so as to show the way, the heavy ring on his finger accidentally smashing into his questioner's mouth.

"Why you—" The other man stepped forward as his friend grabbed for a handkerchief, his intentions plain. Kevin stepped backwards as the poised fist darted towards his stomach, stumbled, fell, his right foot lifting to crack against the other's knee.

Another accident but he felt that explanations would no good. He scrabbled to his feet and ran towards the elevator, making the cage just in time, slamming the door on the man with the bleeding mouth. The drop lifted his stomach to the back of his mouth and he left the cage sweating, fighting the desire to vomit. Weakly he made his way to the street and a welcome cab.

* * * *

He woke to a shriek of pain and stared blankly at the ceiling.

"Damn it!" raved Duncan. "What demon-device have you got in this thing?" He picked up the pillow and threw it across the room. Naturally he had been using the bed. Equally naturally Kevin had been using the floor. So much for promises. Painfully he squinted at the figure of his room-mate looming above him.

"So you're alive," said Duncan. "With the gadgets you use I'm surprised. Or do you consider that electric shocks are good for you?"

"You should have used your own pillow," said Kevin weakly. He tried to sit upright and fell back as a hammer began to pound either temple. "What happened?"

"You came home stinking drunk, that's what happened," snapped Duncan. "I had to pay the cabbie double-rate for the mess you made and for bringing you up. Hell, man, didn't I warn you to stay away from the booze?"

It had been good advice—a pity he hadn't taken it. Kevin rolled, lifted himself to all fours, climbed slowly to his feet. The room swam and he grabbed at the table to steady himself. The pounding in his temples eased a little and he looked around. The clothes he had worn lay in a soiled heap to one side. He was naked, his body itching with dried perspiration.

"Make some coffee," he croaked as he headed towards the shower. "Please."

The shower helped a little but he still felt ghastly when he sat down to sip at the cup Duncan set before him. Parties, he thought.

They were supposed to be fun. Well, to hell with them. From now on he would live a normal, safe, unexciting life.

"Drink this," ordered Duncan. He held out a glass containing milk and slime. "Gulp it right down. It's raw eggs," he explained as Kevin shuddered. "They'll settle your stomach."

"You must be joking."

"Get it down," insisted Duncan. "It'll do you good. I know what I'm talking about."

Too weak to argue Kevin swallowed the mess, gagging as it went down, then sat waiting for the reaction. It surprised him. Instead of immediately bringing up what he had swallowed he felt a little better. The coffee helped more. In a little while, though still queasy, he was strong enough to complete his toilet and dress.

"That's better," approved Duncan. "Now you look almost human. Those clothes will have to be dumped though," he said looking at the discarded heap. "A pity. I liked those things."

"I'll pay for them," promised Kevin. He produced his wallet and blinked at the contents.

"I had to pay off the cabbie," said Duncan quickly. "I told you that. Double-rate and you must have taken a tour of the city. Never mind the clothes," he added as Kevin counted what was left. I guess I'm friend enough to do you a favour."

Some friend, thought Kevin bitterly, but he supposed he should be grateful. After all, Duncan had warned him not to drink. He glanced at his watch and winced, he'd never make it by normal transport, which meant taking another cab. More expense, but, at least, it would give him time for another cup of coffee.

"How did it go?" asked Duncan as he refilled his cup. "Did you make an impression?"

Kevin shrugged. "I did my best."

"Did you pile it on as I advised? Make yourself a character?"

"I think so." Kevin gave a brief resumé as he gulped at the coffee. "At least I didn't disgrace myself. I saved that until I got outside."

"Mixed drinks," said Duncan sagely. "They can be the devil. Delayed action, sort of, they hit you hard, fast and when you least expect it. I remember a girl I took out once, a nice little thing from the record department, she was eager to try everything and I had the money to play along. I figured that I was on to a sure thing. Then, wham! One minute she was all over me, the next she was all over the floor. I had to get out fast before they billed me for the mess. Then there was a time at—"

"Tell me later," interrupted Kevin. "I've got to get going."

Work was a more virulent hell than usual. Somehow managed to get through it until an hour before quitting time when Hepton, grinning like a shark, announced that the floor overseer wanted to see him.

Mr Frobisher was sixty years old, built like a pumpkin, a frustrated executive with a fanatical dedication to efficiency, status, responsibility and awareness of position. He stared at Kevin and then at the papers strewn on his desk.

"Mr Blake," he said, not looking up. "Are you feeling quite well?"

"Yes," said Kevin. "I'm fine."

"You don't look it." Frobisher looked up from the papers. "Do you have a fever, perhaps? Or a cold?"

"No, nothing like that."

"Like what, then?" Frobisher was sharp. "An upset stomach, maybe? A certain queasiness? Are you a drinking man, Mr Blake?"

"I never touch the stuff," said Kevin, wondering what all this was about. "I don't believe that a man should poison himself with such things."

"I am glad to hear it, Mr Blake. I summoned you here because, Mr Hepton reported that he thought you might be sick yesterday. He is also very worried about your efficiency today. It was my duty to check your work and I am very disappointed in what I found. This consignment of shin-guards, for example. They should have been sent to Liramatopsha. Instead you dispatched them to Lyrgista. The inhabitants of that planet," he added gently, "are intelligent worms. Worms are devoid of legs. Tell me, Mr Blake, what possible use could they have for shin-guards?"

Kevin made a helpless gesture. "It was a mistake," he admitted. "The names are very much alike. I guess I slipped up on that one."

"A potentially expensive mistake, Mr Blake."

"I rarely make a mistake at all as my record will show."

"Past performance is no guarantee of future conduct," snapped Frobisher. "The Transworld Trading Company has the right to demand the very best from each of its employees. A man cannot give of his best if his concentration is elsewhere. I am fully aware of your outside interests, Mr Blake. I am also fully aware that a man with an engrossing hobby cannot devote his entire being to any ordinary pursuit. I suggest that it is time you reached a decision—either you devote all your energies to the company which employs you or you devote all your time to your hobby. Do I make myself clear, Mr Blake?"

Too damn clear, thought Kevin. Hepton had slipped in the knife but good and this fat fool was finishing the execution.

Tightly he said: "I think you are going beyond your authority. What I do in my own time has nothing to do with the firm. If you intend to crucify me for a single mistake I must give you due notice that I intend to place the matter before the union."

"As is your privilege," snapped Frobisher. "I have tried to be gentle with you, Blake, but it is apparent that you refuse to see reason. Very well. You are suspended until the result of the enquiry. You will notify the union, I assume? The next meeting of the joint council is in three days' time. Please make yourself available for questioning on noon of that day."

Three days, thought Kevin bitterly as he left the office. The mistake had been his fault so he wouldn't get paid no matter what the result of the enquiry. And Frobisher had a lot of influence, he might get demoted or even canned. Well, to hell with him, it would give him time to work on the book.

* * * *

The next day Ransom phoned and said; "Kevin, boy, just what did you do at that party?" His round face shone from the screen, the tufts of hair in his ears catching the light so that he seemed to be wearing oddly-placed luminescent horns. "Talk," he urged. "You know that you can trust me but I have to know what I'm doing. I can't operate in the dark. That room-mate of yours said that you'd cut quite a swath. Can he be trusted?"

Kevin was cautious. "Why?"

"Never mind the questions, boy, just give me the facts. Remember that I'm working for you all the time. Is it true that you killed a man down in Lower Tallahassee?"

"What?" Kevin scowled. "Did Duncan say that?"

"And what about that business in Peru?"

"Listen," snapped Kevin. "I don't know what this is all about but I've never been to Peru and I wouldn't know Lower Tallahassee if I saw it. That nurd's been putting you on."

"You can trust me, boy," soothed Ransom. "I'm your agent, remember? I don't give a damn if you killed a regiment and salted them down for beef. It's just that I've got to have the facts. Is it true that you met your second wife in a bordello?"

"Sure," said Kevin sarcastically. "I married her for her money and quit when she wanted me to take an active part in the business."

"That's the spirit, boy," said Ransom enthusiastically. "There's nothing like detail to flesh out a character. Can you be at my office at ten tomorrow morning?"

"Why?"

"You keep asking questions," complained the agent. "Why don't you just leave everything to me? I'm plugging, selling, pushing you all the time. All you have to carry the ball. Just leave all the thinking to me. I won't let you down."

"Wait a minute!" yelled Kevin. "What the hell's this all about?"

He was talking to a dead screen. Impatiently he found coins, fed the device, punched the number. It was engaged. Scowling he recovered his money and returned to his work. The scattered sheets of paper had lost their appeal. Even the case history of a convent girl who had taken two drinks and found herself in an embarrassing situation with two men and a dog failed to revive his enthusiasm. The drinks would have to be altered to a shot of mescalin, of course, and the dog eliminated because of the Canine Defence League, but what remained would fill at least a page. Bleakly he made the necessary alterations and tossed the sheet on one of the heaps.

At times writing could be hell.

Maybe he should go for a walk, he thought. Get out away from the room and the heaps of paper, mix with people and look at the sky. He was becoming too introspective and the new book didn't help. Julia had been harder to handle than ever when he'd collected the latest batch of selections. It had been a mistake to choose such a subject, already she was more than hinting that personal research would be necessary in order to verify the old histories and with hallucinogens on free sale it was getting difficult to refuse.

And that character at the party had shaken him with his knowledge of the source material for Survival in Society. It had been a near thing even though he had managed to talk his way out of it. Perhaps that was why he had hit the booze immediately afterwards. And now Ransom was asking crazy questions.

Duncan, of course, the nurd was gilding the lily, getting a kick out of building a phoney character. But who could have done the asking?

"A girl," said Duncan blandly when he arrived home and Kevin asked the question. "A nice dish with figure to match. Long hair, earrings and a thing hanging around her neck. She said she was writing a series of articles on contemporary authors and wanted some background. Naturally I gave it to her. She bought the drinks too," he added. "We had quite a time."

"Her name?"

"Eagan, I think. Claudia Eagan. Was she at the party?" He grinned as Kevin nodded. "That's what I figured. You hit the bell there, friend, and made them curious. So I fed them a little meat."

Claudia? Kevin frowned as he thought about it but it made a weird kind of sense. She had certainly told Felicita about his fictitious wives but why would she be checking up? And how had Ransom known what Duncan had said?

"I don't know," said Duncan when he asked. "But this could be interesting. You've got to meet your agent at ten tomorrow?"

"That's what he said."

"And you don't know why?"

"No."

"I've got a feeling there might be something in the air," said Duncan thoughtfully. "Maybe Felicita Marmot's keen to become your patron and wants to launch a big publicity campaign for your next book. She'd want to get the background right and would naturally do a little checking. But don't worry. I haven't let you down. It was like feeding candy to a child. Each time she mentioned something I piled it higher but kept it vague enough so as to maintain the mystery."

"I'll bet," said Kevin.

"Sure I did. I'm used to handling people, remember?" Duncan glanced at his watch. "I'd tell you about it but your time is up. Sorry, pal, but the room's all mine and I'm expecting company. You're on your way, yes?"

"No," said Kevin firmly. "Not until you've told what sort of lies you fed to that girl."

* * * *

Ransom had two rooms in a basement; one where he lived, the other where he conducted his business. It held decent furniture, framed testimonials and a wall completely with well-bound books. Filing cabinets, a phone, a concealed bar and a projector completed the equipment. It gave the unobtrusive impression of a man successful at his trade and, thought Kevin, it was no lie. Ransom was clever, handling anything in the artistic line which would sell, and most of the time he could be trusted not to sell his clients short.

He waved Kevin to a chair, beaming; radiating confidence. "You're in good time, Kevin, boy. I like that. In our profession time is money. How is the new book coming along?"

"Not too bad," said Kevin. "It deals with the hidden dangers of—"

"Don't tell me," Ransom interrupted. "I'll read it when it's done. No need for double-work if you can help it, is there? Didn't I tell you that Survival In Society has been selected by Stellar Snappies as their give-away book of the week? No money, of course, but the prestige, boy. The prestige!"

Kevin said; "How about off-world sales?"

"That's a hard market, Kevin, boy. A few to the libraries, of course, the usual standing order, but nothing in the reprint line as yet. But don't worry. It'll come as sure as fate. It's just a matter of waiting." He leaned forward, lowering his voice. "And now, boy, what about that man in Lower Tallahassee?"

"Nothing about him, he's dead."

"And that business in Peru?"

"Nothing about that either," snapped Kevin. "Look, is that why you asked me here? To throw a lot of questions? What's this all about?"

"I think," said a voice behind him. "I can explain that better than your agent."

Paul Tarvainen stepped into view and calmly sat down.

From Ransom's expression Kevin guessed that the visitor was unexpected. Tarvainen confirmed the suspicion.

"I know that your arrangement was that you should fetch your client to my hotel," he said to the agent. "But I thought it better to be here when he arrived. As it is I seem to be a little late."

Ransom made a quick recovery. "Just as you prefer, Mr Tarvainen, sir. I would have suggested it myself but your instructions were plain. Your hotel at noon. However, Mr Blake and I had a little business to discuss. About his book," he explained. "An agent must work in close collaboration with his—"

Tarvainen cut off the flow with an imperious gesture. "I am interested in you, Blake. Your book intrigued me and I wanted to meet its author. It was at my instigation that you were invited to the party. I was not disappointed in what I saw."

Kevin glanced at Ransom who made a helpless gesture. He's had no time to brief me, thought Kevin with sudden understanding. Tell me the part he wanted me to play. But it was obvious from what Tarvainen had said what that part should be. He expected to meet the same character he had at the party. Well, Kevin was willing to oblige.

Curtly he said; "I assume there's some point to all this?"

"Be patient," snapped Tarvainen. "I have a proposition to make, but first let me congratulate you on the way you handled those two men I had waiting for you. It was a test, I admit, but I had to be certain of the kind of man you are. Attack and a quick, strategic retreat, it was neatly done. I have no doubt that you could have killed them both had you wished."

For a moment Kevin wondered what the hell the man was talking about, then he remembered the incident when he'd left the party. The loungers, the unfortunate accidents, his desperate flight.

They would have inflated the episode to boost their own reputation. Silence, he decided, was the best policy.

"But, of course," continued Tarvainen after a moment, "you did not wish. Why should you? To kill them would have meant investigation and awkward questions. But enough of that. I'll come to the point, Blake. I need a man. A very special kind of man and I think you could be what I'm looking for. Your book shows a great depth of insight into the mechanics of survival and your reputation, what I have learned of it, bolsters the fact that you are tough, shrewd, hard, versatile, adaptive and intelligent. Will you work for me?"

Ransom cleared his throat. "A moment, Mr Tarvainen, as Kevin's agent I handle all business matters on his behalf. If you will tell me the nature of the proposed employment together with the remuneration you have in mind I'll get busy drawing up a contractual agreement."

Kevin said; "Doing what?"

"Bring my daughter back home to Earth where she belongs," said Tarvainen. "She is a sweet girl but wilful, I'm afraid, easily swayed by undesirable acquaintances. I simply want you to go after her and bring her back. I am not a poor man," he added. "I will pay expenses and a large bonus on successful completion of the assignment."

"I'll handle the financial side, Kevin, boy," said Ransom hastily.

Kevin ignored him, frowning. "This doesn't make sense. I suppose your daughter is of age?"

"Naturally."

"Then she doesn't have to do anything she doesn't want."

"Legally, no," admitted Tarvainen. "But is it necessary to worry about trifles like that? I want her back, Blake, and I'm willing to pay for the service. The details I leave to you, I am interested only in results, and you seem particularly well-equipped to handle any little difficulty which could arise."

"He'll do it, Mr Tarvainen," said Ransom quickly. "Subject to my approval as to the remuneration, of course. Now if we could just get together on—"

"Wait a minute," snapped Kevin. At times Ransom was a little too eager. "Let's not rush into this." He stared at Tarvainen. "You haven't waited this long to fetch her back," he accused. "You must have had others working on it. How come they haven't delivered the goods?"

"They failed, Blake. They had no guts. Two men of the Haul 'em Home agency located her on Glamis II where she had become a temporary adoptee of the Venshi tribe. On my behalf they offered the chief ten tons of beads, paint, feathers and bone if he would deliver her, unharmed, into their care. He agreed but pointed out that the girl had placed herself under the protection of the tribe-champion. First they would have to beat him in single, unarmed combat. The champion," he added, "was a product of the Kin-Chow laboratories. Nine feet tall, three-fifty pounds, able to bend a two-inch thick iron bar in his bare hands. The cowards refused to meet him."

Ransom made tutting noises. Kevin held his tongue.

"It's been like that on a dozen worlds," continued Tarvainen. "Always she manages to elude capture—I mean persuasion. I'm no longer young, Blake. My health isn't what it should be. I long to see my little girl again before it is too late."

"Cut off her money," suggested Kevin. "Or has she enough of her own?"

"She is financially independent. How soon will you be ready to leave?"

"Almost immediately," said Ransom.

"Now wait a minute," protested Kevin. "I haven't agreed to anything yet. Just how many of your agents have managed to get themselves killed?"

"That doesn't matter," said Ransom quickly, the hairs in his ears bristling at the scent of money. "They weren't like you, Kevin, boy. They didn't have your specialised knowledge of how to survive in various societies. That's what Mr Tarvainen's buying, a specialist who can guarantee success. And he's willing to pay well for such a man. Right, Mr Tarvainen?"

"On a contingent basis, yes."

Ransom beamed. "There you are, Kevin, boy. What have you got to worry about?"

A lot, thought Kevin sourly. There was too much he didn't know and if experts at the game had failed how could he hope to do better? On the other hand the prospect was tempting. An off-world vacation would get him away from Frobisher, the job, Julia and that damned book. And he didn't have to stick his neck out. Just travel around for a while and then make a discreet return.

Tarvainen mistook his brooding silence. "There will be basic expenses, naturally."

"And something on account," said Ransom firmly. "But you can leave all that to me, Kevin, boy. Now you just go home and settle what has to be done. I'll call you as soon as Mr Tarvainen signs the contract."

CHAPTER 4

There was the usual crowd at the spaceport. Neatly dressed in his travelling gear of knee-boots, laminated pants and blouse of discreet lavender, a scarlet cummerbund and long jacket to match, Kevin hefted his briefcase and looked sourly at the motley collection of men, women and children all loaded with various bundles and bales. To hell with it, he decided, this was no way to start an adventure. Tarvainen's money could buy him VIP service.

As he turned away a weasel-faced man wearing faded chartreuse sidled close.

"You wanna place close to the head of the line, mister? A good spot going cheap."

Kevin hesitated. "What do you call cheap?"

"He's been waiting ten hours. Call it five an hour, uh?"

"Call it four," suggested Kevin.

"Four-fifty?"

"It's a deal." Kevin followed the man to where a withered oldster patiently stood in line and paid over the cash as he took his place. The oldster coughed, took his cut and promptly moved back to the end of the queue to resume his occupation. A woman at Kevin's rear snorted.

"Some people," she said acidly. "They think money can buy anything."

Kevin ignored her.

"That's the trouble with this stinking world," she continued. "No ethics. No consideration for others. It's grab, grab all the time."

"Knock it off," said her husband. He was bowed beneath the weight of a pack, carried a bundle suspended from his neck and hefted a heavy case in each hand. "He didn't create the system so don't blame him for taking advantage of it. She's just tired," he said to Kevin as the woman snorted again and stalked off towards a bank of vending machines. You want coffee?"

"Thanks."

"Make it three, Lorna!" the man yelled. "A good woman," he said as she waved and took her place in the line. "A real worker. She'll be worth her weight in gold on Lachise."

"The Erianda system?"

"That's right. You know it?" He sighed as Kevin shook his head. "Maybe we're taking a chance but anything's better than staying here. I'm a carpenter," he explained. "A lousy trade but I'm stuck with it. And who the hell can afford real wood? I tell you, mister, if it wasn't for repairs I'd have been broke years ago." He set down the cases. "Here comes the coffee."

Two hours later they reached emigration and Kevin filed into one of the slots. Ahead of him a man yelled, despairingly, "It's a mistake, I tell you! The damn computer's got it wrong! I don't owe nothing to no one. You've got to let me through!"

"Knock it off," snapped the weary official and slapped a button. The floor fell from beneath the protester's feet and he went wailing down the chute leading to egress. "Next!"

Kevin stepped forward.

"Gimme your iden." The official dropped the card into a slot and grunted when the light flashed green. "OK, you're clear, no debts, unpaid taxes, pending court actions or criminal charges." He handed back the card. "What are you carrying?"

"Papers." Kevin unzipped the briefcase and showed the contents.

"Travelling light, uh? Well, that's your business." The official drew a deep breath. "Do you fully realise that once you leave Earth you are outside the boundaries of its jurisdiction and that you cannot claim welfare or any assistance from any Terrestrial Embassy, Consul or Commercial House as a distressed person and that any marriage to an alien will not make either your partner or any children a citizen of this planet and that if you take part in any actual or implied act of aggression against this world or any of its possessions you will be liable to summary execution on capture?"

"I do," said Kevin.

"Right, on your way. Next!"

Beyond the emigration shed a hundred-foot wall topped with spikes, spines and electrified wire completely surrounded the landing field. Inside was pandemonium.

"Step this way!" clacked a man-high turtle with a gemmed carapace. "Free transport to Woomis! Guaranteed employment! Good recreation! Free transport! Free food while in transit! Free entertainment from our qualified ship-girl! Free drinks! Roll up! Roll up! Two more places vacant! Don't miss this wonderful opportunity!"

Next to the turtle a thing like a gorilla wearing a vermillion codpiece, spangled robe and a plug hat beat on a drum and chanted, sonorously; "Ride on the *Vermis*. All planets of the Rigellian system. Low rates, maximum comfort, leaving almost immediately. Galactic certificate of spaceworthiness on display!"

"Direct transit to Arcturus!" shrieked another creature. "Full meals provided! Minors half-price, babes in arms free!"

"Free water!" screamed a thing like a wilted lettuce. "High humidity! Artificial rain! Travel in luxury to the worlds of Procyon!"

A mobile barrel with legs and tendrils verberated: "Cheap travel on the *Cask*! Goods taken in part exchange! Indentures accepted! Ride now and pay later!"

Kevin halted, staring at the assembled touts, looking beyond them to where their ships, ball-shaped, cone-shaped, polyhedron, cigar, dumbell, star, finned, planed, painted and battered rested on the field. One took off as he watched, blue radiance shimmering, a distant thunderclap echoing as it vanished. The turtle, seeing his indecision, came scampering over.

"Wondering where to go, sir? Come to Woomis. Free transport in return for a short six months of labour in pleasant mines fitted with every labour-saving device. Easy, delightful work digging precious zylis crystals and you keep ten percent of all you produce. Sign up now, sir, before you miss this wonderful opportunity!"

"You'll regret it if you do," said a deep voice before Kevin could refuse. It belonged to a roundly fat, plump smiling man who wore a voluminous cloak and steeple hat covered with a multitude of signs, flags, symbols and insignia. "Food comes dear when you're stuck at the bottom of a mine and it'll cost all you earn to pay for it."

"You malign me!" clacked the turtle angrily. "You throw doubt on my integrity. I've a mind to complain to the Association. Must I remind you of the Prime Ethic of the Galactic Federation?"

"Caveat emptor," said the fat man. "Let the buyer beware or, in other words, let each fool take care of himself." Companionably he took Kevin's arm and led him from the snapping turtle. "He'll get over it," he said. "But you've had a lucky escape, my friend. May I introduce myself? I am Magister Melavian of the Terrestrial Travellers Aid Society. We are a charitable organisation whose work it is to give help and advice to all of our planet who are in need of it. We exist," he added meaningfully, "by the voluntary donations of those to whom we have been of service."

"And very nice too," said Kevin.

"Had you signed that contract you would have doomed yourself to a lifetime of endless labour, my friend. I am happy to have been the means to have saved you from such a fate."

"Virtue," said Kevin blandly, "is it's own reward."

Melavian breathed deeply. "You are a gentleman," he said. "A person of sincerity and understanding. One who would not begrudge a small donation to a worthy cause. I may have been of assistance to you. I shall certainly be of assistance to others. But a man must eat, my friend. A man must live."

"Yes," said Kevin shortly, staring at his self-appointed benefactor. "But sometimes I wonder why."

* * * *

Escaping Melavian's curses he found refuge in a glass-walled cafeteria, waiting patiently as a warted pineapple selected a dish of chopped worms, trying not to let the spiny rustle of a mobile cactus behind him disturb his attention. Armed with coffee and cake he found a vacant seat and settled down to plan his next move. Ransom had supplied him with a dossier on the missing girl and he opened it, studying the photograph of his quarry. She was quite a dish. Tall, lissom, with a mane of blonde hair and a figure which swelled in all the right places. The face had the imperious look of a spoiled brat or a natural-born queen. There was fire, there, he decided, and arrogance, and more than a touch of wilfulness. And maybe she was a little crazy, how else to explain her disregard of parental instruction?

Her actions since she had left Earth bolstered his suspicion. A taxi dancer on Frendis V, married to a six-set on Ghiase, a ship-girl on a Venadian freighter, restaurant owner on Jhalen, breeder of Butashglian snails, wail-singer on Shlem... The list seemed endless. A girl trying to find herself. A poor little rich kid who sought her proper niche. A pain in the neck if you happened to be close but, at the moment, a paid vacation as far as he was concerned.

Happily Kevin put down the papers and reached for his coffee and cake. He'd go through the motions he decided. He might even catch up with her and ask her to be a good girl and come back home. That was if she happened to be somewhere approachable, of course, he was damned if he was going to hunt her through slime and mould, burst his eardrums with ultra-sonic caterwauling or have to fight some mutated ape to the death for the privilege of taking her by the hand.

"Mind if I sit here?"

Startled at the unusual courtesy Kevin looked up at the man who had spoken. He was middle-aged, with the heavy features and drooping lids of a bloodhound, soberly dressed in blue and gold. He held a plate of lumbuki and a cup of steaming tvass.

"Sure," said Kevin. "Help yourself."

The man grunted and, sitting, began to devour his food with wolf-like concentration. Kevin stared out of the window at the constant stream of emigrants pouring into the area. Most knew where they were going and headed directly towards the line of waiting vessels. Others shopped around for bargains among the clamouring touts. From time to time a ship rose in a shimmer of blue, others settling to take their place.

"Look at them," said the man. He pushed away his empty plate. "Like ants. God, I'd forgotten there was this many people in the galaxy." He reached for his cup of tvass. "Thomas," he said. "Talfryn Thomas. You?"

Kevin blinked but gave his name adding; "You just shipping out?"

"Not just," said Talfryn, "but shipping out, yes. I first left fifteen years ago. I came back a week since to try and talk my kid brother into joining me. I've a farm on Kappa Thuban. A good place with wood, beasts and running water. I can't wait to get back."

"And your brother?"

"He won't move," said Talfryn disgustedly. "I've worn my throat sore telling him the advantages but the nurd won't shift. He's got a box in a tower, two rooms and a kitchen, a bathroom you can't turn around in and it takes twenty minutes to reach the ground."

"A nice place," said Kevin. "He's lucky."

"Lucky? Hell, I could build him a place twice as good as that with his own land and all conveniences. But would he shift? Like hell he would. Told me he has a secure job and likes things as they are. No guts, that's what, and I told him so to his face. No spirit. No enterprise. Well, to hell with him." Talfryn gulped at his tvass. "He's soft," he said broodingly lowering the cup. "Like most of the people of this damned planet."

"Maybe not," protested Kevin.

Talfryn grunted. "Then why don't they leave, uh? You tell me that. There's plenty of room out there." His arm gestured towards the sky. "Billions of worlds where a man can get along if he's willing to work. Work and keep his nose clean and doesn't step on anyone's toes. Or claws," he added, "or fins, flippers, paws, webs, hoofs or what have you. People get along. No matter what they look like they get along. Earth's crammed to the bursting point, so why don't they leave?"

Because they didn't want to, thought Kevin, most of them anyway. They liked what they had and didn't want to swap it for something they weren't sure of. Crowding wasn't so bad when you were used to it and everyone on Earth was. At least you were never alone.

Fifty years, he thought, looking out of the window. That's how long ago it had been since it had happened. The first trading ship of the Galactic Federation had contained intelligent lobsters which had been shot on sight. The next held humanoids, blue-skinned, true, but enough like men to get a hearing. They had traded a load of hundred carat diamonds for machine tools, rabbit-fur slippers and a herd of dairy-milk cows. Then had come the deluge with ships falling like rain and spaceports opening in every country. To the traders Earth was a bonanza and they came from all over. In five years the planet was an accepted member of the Federation.

"You shipping out?" Talfryn was abrupt. "Maybe."

"You're cautious," said the outworlder. "All you Earthsiders are and I keep forgetting. Where I come from a man likes to know something about the people he meets. And maybe I could be of help. Where are you bound?"

"Illagesh." That was the latest information Kevin had on the girl's whereabouts. "You know it?"

Talfryn scowled. "Hell, man, the galaxy's a big place. Can't you do better than that? What sun does it circle?"

Kevin dug into his papers. "Keelab. Number X31 in the guide."

"Still no help. I've never heard of the place but, from the number, it's way out in the back of beyond. You know how you're going to get there?"

"I'll manage."

"Sure you will, but take some advice. Free," Talfryn said quickly as Kevin hesitated. "Ride on a humanoid ship if you can get one. It's no fun travelling with a load of bladders, puffballs or insects. And make sure you get a firm contract before you leave. Luck."

"Luck," said Kevin, and finished the last of his coffee and cake.

* * * *

The information bureau was a madhouse of yelling emigrants and harassed officials, even the automatic machines seemed to be smoking at the terminals. Kevin gave the installation one glance and decided to make his own way. Dodging the touts he moved towards the ships. A jellyfish enclosed in a plastic envelope surged forward.

"Sir?" It said liquidly. "You seek transport, sir? Very fine ship awaits your pleasure. Suit provided for air-breathers. All home comforts."

"You going to X311875?"

"A moment, sir." Tentacles riffled a thick volume. "Regretfully no, sir. But touch down on many worlds of great interest. Reduced rates for long journey."

"No, thanks," said Kevin.

"Suggest you tranship at Ophidia, sir. Big spaceport with many vessels. Special rate for journey. You sign?"

Shaking his head Kevin proceeded down the line. A fern waved at him, a giant mantis clicked its claws, what seemed to be a rusty dustbin hooted to attract his attention. Impatiently Kevin lifted his voice.

"X311875!" he yelled. "Is anyone going to X311875?"

Two hours later when, hoarse and weary he was nearing the end of the line, a seven-foot girl, scaled and with a crested skull, hissed at him from the foot of a loading ramp.

"We pass close to desired star, sir. Ten lights, main depot for area, short journey. Mail and supply ship take you rest of way."

Kevin slowed, doubting if he could do better. "All right," he said. "How much?"

Money paid and details arranged the stewardess led him into the main cabin. It was full of seats in which bulked various masses of fur, feather and scale. A familiar face beamed at him as he approached the vacant seat at its side.

"Well, well," said Talfryn. "Talk about coincidence! This is great! Nothing like having another human along to shorten a journey. Do you get off before me or after?"

"Damned if I know," said Kevin, sitting and easing his aching legs. "I've got to tranship anyway. The nearest they get is ten lights."

"Nothing to it," said Talfryn. "You can spit that distance." He frowned, thinking. "You must get off after me," he decided. "I know the route pretty well to where I'm going and I've no memory of Keelab. You got business there?"

Kevin hesitated then made up his mind. It would do no harm to tell the man what he was after. It might, with luck, shorten his quest and he had to start work sometime. It might as well be now. He unzipped his briefcase.

"I'm looking for a woman," he said, producing the photograph. "Crystal Tarvainen. Do you know her?"

"No," said Talfryn regretfully. "But I sure wish I did."

"Have you heard of her then?"

"Not on my world." The farmer looked at the print and sucked in his cheeks. "Man, I could really do with a woman like that! I'd give ten years' crops to find one just like her. Just think of the little woman waiting at home while you were out working," he said dreamily. "Getting your grub ready, sewing your clothes, sorting the seed. Damn it, if I had a wife like that I'd make her wear gloves. I'd keep her out of the sun. I wouldn't let her do a thing she didn't have to do. You married?"

"No," said Kevin.

"She your girl?"

"I'm just looking for her."

"When you find her bring her to my place," said Talfryn. "I'd build you a house just so as I could look at her now and again. Are you a drinking man, friend?"

Kevin blinked at the abrupt change of subject. "Well, not exactly."

"It helps," said Talfryn with the wisdom of the experienced traveller. "It so happens that I've got a little something with me. A bottle for emergencies. I guess that a toast to the little lady wouldn't come amiss." He delved into his capacious valise. "You'll join me?"

Kevin joined him. Half-way through the second drink he felt the seat lurch a little and guessed they were on their way. Two hours later with the bottle empty and his fellow passenger who had drunk most of it fast asleep the stewardess came round with trays each bearing a slab of something and a cup of water.

"Your first transit meal, sir," she explained. "If you wish something a little more succulent it can be provided at a slight extra charge. You wish?"

Kevin shook his head, bit into the slab and chewed with determination. It had the consistency of cheese and tasted of seaweed but he forced it down. The meal over he went exploring, found what he was looking for and washed his hands before returning to the cabin. A group of humans were playing cards. Two avians and a serpent hissed and twittered as they threw dice. A thing like a bear grumbled softly to itself as it read a book. The rest stared fixedly at the wall of the cabin where a screen displayed a hypnotic, sleep-inducing pattern of constantly changing colour.

The romance of interstellar travel, thought Kevin sourly, and returning to his chair stared at the screen until he fell asleep.

He jerked awake to find the stewardess at his side.

"We have arrived at Vebgal, sir," she informed him. "Gamma world of the Vidpar system. We shall remain there for five hours. If you wish to leave the ship you must have prophylactic injections against leaf-rot, scale-mould and mange."

"No thanks," said Kevin.

"The cost is most reasonable."

"No."

"It is a most interesting world," urged the girl. "The tree-folk manufacture various items of great value and charm and are able to discourse on matters of philosophy and science. For a modest outlay you will be able to study their homes, temples and the manner in which they rear their young. Make the most of your travels, sir! Gain experiences which will fill your later days!"

Firmly Kevin shook his head and turned to see Talfryn's grinning face.

"They try," said the farmer. "For profit, naturally. They've got an arrangement with the local tribe and get a cut of the proceeds. But if ever you leave the ship make sure you get back on time. They won't wait a second even if they see you coming." He stretched. "How about another bottle?"

Kevin hesitated, he didn't want to encourage expensive habits.

"You might as well," said Talfryn. "There's damn all else to do."

Time became a succession of eating, drinking and sleeping the whole thing adding up to screaming boredom. At intervals they landed when the ritual of offering package deals and guided tours was repeated. At one of the halts Talfryn rose, stretched and said; "Home, by God! It'll be a long day before I go wandering again. Good luck, friend, and I hope you find your girl. Don't forget to visit when you do."

His place was taken by a plump matron who insisted on telling Kevin all about the romantic difficulties of her youngest daughter and the peculiar illness a friend of hers had contracted on an amorous adventure to a neighbouring planet. Two things about which Kevin couldn't have cared less.

She was followed after a mercifully short interval by a large, talkative snail who demanded to know whether Kevin adhered to the dogma of the Universal One.

"It is so terribly important," it said, gnashing its toothless mouth, eyes glaring from extended stalks. "The most primitive of all intelligent life-forms must surely see that. After all, if Universal Intelligence is the attribute of the Universal One, and if we all share in that intelligence as we surely must, then it becomes obvious that you and I are basically the same creature. Two differently shaped cells of the Universal Body, each a fragment of the Universal Mind. We use the brains of the structures in which we find ourselves, but we are no more separate entities than are the individual scales of my body or the individual fingers of your hands. You agree?"

"Yes," said Kevin, trying not to sound harassed. "How could I refute your logic?"

"Not my logic," corrected the snail gently. "The obvious truth of the Universal One. But I knew that you would agree that, at last, all intelligent creatures can grasp the concept of the Universal Truth. You are from Earth?"

Kevin nodded.

"A most interesting place so I have been told," continued the snail. "Though I have heard an unpleasant rumour that certain of your tribes actually eat members of my species. A revolting canard, naturally."

"A disgusting lie!"

"I am glad to hear you say so. To be eaten," the snail mused. "To be boiled, removed from one's shell, rolled in animal fats and flavoured with pungent herbs. Then to be eaten." It gave a small shudder. "A most distressing concept and yet, when one thinks about it, it is all a part of the Universal Experience. A part of me, that is a segment of the Universal Mind, is most probably being eaten at this very moment. As is a part of you also, my friend. We have to be philosophical about such matters, do we not?"

As well as everything else, thought Kevin grimly, as the creature chattered on. It was the only way to remain sane.

CHAPTER 5

Illagesh was a pleasant world with soaring mountains and rolling seas, thick forests and plains verdant beneath a G-type sun. Like Earth must have been at one time, mused Kevin as he stared through his hotel window. Natural and unspoiled, the air free of poison, the sunshine undimmed by smog. There would be seasons, he thought, snow in winter and frost, cool breezes from the sea and the warm, basking heat of summer.

He inhaled and reluctantly turned from the window. His room was soft, clean and luxurious, a pleasant change from the one he had occupied at the depot while waiting ten days for the shuttle. But now he was finally here and rested, bathed and refreshed he was ready for work.

At least, he told himself, the pretence of it. Tarvainen would expect a report and would know from where it came. He would go about, ask some questions, go fishing perhaps and then he would see. He might even write a book, a real one, dealing with his adventures, perhaps. It might even be possible to get a contract from the local chamber of commerce to publicise the planet. In the meantime he'd better get on with the job.

Unzipping his briefcase he stared again at the photograph of Crystal Tarvainen. It was beginning to get him. She looked so soft, so beautiful; so interestingly feminine. Her eyes, as they stared from the print, seemed to catch and hold his own. He would find her, he decided, if only to say hello.

He lowered the photograph as someone knocked and opened the door. It was the chambermaid, a local girl, practically human aside from her pointed ears and cat-pupiled eyes. Her skin was a dusky olive and painted toenails gleamed from beneath the hem of her embroidered robe. Little bells tinkled musically from her graceful arms.

"Your pardon, sir," she apologised. "If you wish to breakfast in your room it can be arranged. If not the service has now commenced below."

"I'll go down," said Kevin. Impulsively he held out the photograph. "Do you know this girl? Have you seen her?"

Her eyes dropped to the print, lifted. "No, sir. Yes, sir."

"You don't know her," said Kevin, guessing. "But you've seen her. Is that it?"

"Yes, sir."

"Does she live here in the city?"

"I do not know, sir. Will you descend to eat now?"

The dining room was almost filled with a scatter of Terrestrials and natives of both sexes, the men tall, brawny, armed with ornamented knives. Kevin found a vacant table and concentrated on the fruit, fish and juices which a waiter served. Broodingly he considered his next move. It was pointless to ask around at random, he decided. It would be best to go directly to someone who should have the information.

Outside the hotel he looked around. The streets were wide, clean and lightly filled with traffic. A few electric cars, some carts drawn by animals, rickshaws each with a pair of runners. A glaring sign guided him to the local bank. The clerk, a native, was firm.

"I regret, sir, that no information about any of our clients can be divulged."

Kevin restrained his temper. "Let me see the manager."

The manager was more loquacious but just as firm.

"Mr Blake, you must realise that there are certain ethics which we of the profession must struggle to maintain. It would be completely wrong for us to give information about anyone to any stranger who happens to ask." He glanced pointedly at his watch. "Is there anything else, Mr Blake?"

"Yes," said Kevin. "Is there an inquisitor in the area? A prober," he explained. "Someone who can find out things?"

"Such individuals are not encouraged on Illagesh," said the manager coldly. "If you are such a person I strongly advise you to avoid advertising the fact. On this planet privacy is a valued commodity. The door, Mr Blake. Please close it behind you."

At the communications centre a Terrestrial grinned and said; "You too? What gives with this dame?"

"Has someone else been asking after her?"

"Sure. We had a character in here a short while back. I couldn't help him but I told him where to go." He paused significantly. "Thanks," he said as Kevin, recognising the signs, did the necessary. "Try the factor. Old man Finch has lived here for years. Treat him right and he could help a lot."

Finch was a sagging oldster with shrewd eyes and a waspish disposition. He sniffed at Kevin's neat appearance and waved him towards a chair.

"You're new," he said. "Fresh from Earth. Right?"

Kevin admitted it.

"I can always tell," said Finch. "Babes begging for trouble. Take my advice and watch what you say while you're on Illagesh. The natives have a funny habit of taking you literally. Threaten to kill one and he'll kill you first and get away with it on the grounds of self-defence. What do you want?" He grinned when Kevin told him. "Crystal Tarvainen, eh? Well, I can't blame you, she's quite a girl."

"You know her?"

"We've met. Why do you want to find her?"

"I've a message for her," said Kevin, inventing rapidly. "I'm a lawyer acting on behalf of her father. He's dying," he added truthfully, everyone was dying from the moment they were born. "And he wants to see her before he goes."

"Is that the truth?"

"Of course. It's a matter of inheritance. As you know Mr Tarvainen's a very wealthy man and Crystal is his only relative. He loves her, Mr Finch, and he wants to see her. If you know where she is I plead with you to let me know. An old man," he added, "longing to see his little girl for perhaps the last time. A dying man, Mr Finch, you must help him if you can."

"A lawyer," said Finch thoughtfully. "Is that what you are?"

Kevin nodded, stuck with the lie. And it seemed to have been a good one. People respected lawyers and it might give him the edge on the mysterious character who was sniffing after the same quarry.

A bounty-hunter, he guessed. One of Tarvainen's agents who was after the big money. He would be doing her a favour if he kept her out of his hands.

"I can use a lawyer," mused Finch. "Or rather Malvern can."

"Malvern?"

"A man who was asking after Crystal last month. He's got himself into trouble. I don't go much for the helping hand business but I don't like to see an Earthman in a mess if I can help it."

"Never mind him," said Kevin. "What about Crystal? Where can I find her?"

"I don't know. The last I heard of her was that she had a place in the Blue Hills but that was some time ago. Malvern could tell you, though. He went after her. Help him and you could help yourself. You'll find him in jail," he added. "It's the building next to the hospital."

* * * *

It was a three-storied structure with iron bars and a nose-biting smell. A group of uniformed natives stood in the front office all armed with clubs and knives. One of them looked at Kevin as he hesitated in the entrance.

"You want something, sir?"

"Information about a prisoner you have here. A man named Malvern."

"A moment, sir. The sergeant will attend you."

They were polite, at least, thought Kevin as the man guided him towards a desk behind which sat a grizzled official. Thoughtfully he scratched one of his pointed ears.

"Dale Malvern? The Terrestrial?"

"That's right."

"And you want to see him? Why?"

"I'm a lawyer," said Kevin patiently. "I might be able to help."

"A lawyer? An advocate, you mean?"

"I guess that's what you'd call it. I might be able to act on his behalf. What's the charge?"

"He's on preventive detention waiting a court decision as to the determination of an oral contract," said the sergeant. "Well, I guess you might as well have a word with him. Cell 37. Shleeb!"

A turnkey came forward and escorted Kevin up a flight of stairs, along a passage and to where a man sat on a cot in one of a row of cells. He wasn't an attractive sight. His eyes were heavily pouched, his cheeks mottled with broken capillaries and his clothes were a mess. He looked up as the turnkey unlocked the cell and closed the door behind Kevin.

"Thank God for the sight of a human face! Have you got a drink?"

"No."

"They'll get you a bottle if you can pay for it," said Malvern. Did Finch send you?"

"He told me that you were here," said Kevin cautiously.

"Good old Finch! One thing I always say, you can trust a man who holds his liquor, and he certainly can. How about that bottle?"

"Forget the booze," snapped Kevin. "I want to talk about Crystal Tarvainen. How do I find her?"

"You're after her, eh?" Malvern's eyes grew cunning. "Did her old man send you out direct or are you just a freelance?"

"I am operating under the direct instructions of Mr Tarvainen himself," said Kevin stiffly. "I have a most important message to deliver to his daughter. If you can give me any assistance I am sure that he will be only too pleased to help you in your difficulty. Now, if you will tell me how to find her I'll get out of here."

"Not so fast," said Malvern. "I've got to think about this." He sat on the cot and puffed out his cheeks. "Crystal Tarvainen," he mused. "And you want to find her. You come straight from her daddy which means that you be on expenses with a fat bonus for handing her over. Right?"

He grinned as Kevin made no comment. "You don't have to tell me," he said. "I get the picture. And you aren't the first one with that idea. At least six of the boys have chanced their arm but I was lucky. I managed to get away all in one piece. Have you any idea what you're up against? Illagesh isn't like the city, you know. Most of it is pretty rough with wild animals and wilder men. She's managed to tame a few up in the Blue Hills. You can get there all right, but there's no guarantee you'll ever get back. As I said I was lucky.

It took all I had to outfit an expedition and hire guides. Now I'm broke. You get the picture?"

"You're breaking my heart," said Kevin. "What's to stop me hiring your old guides?"

"You could try."

"I could do more than that."

"Sure you could, but no matter what you did you'd end up the same way. Face down in the dirt or in the stomach of some beast. Fresh guy," sneered Malvern. "Straight from good old Mother Earth. You're all the same. I've been out here twenty years learning how to survive and you come out and know it all. Go ahead. Do it the hard way. What do I care? It's your funeral."

He's conning me, thought Kevin, but even so Malvern made sense. What did he know of the wilderness? Hell, he'd never even seen a forest at close hand. How did you find your way when surrounded by trees? What did you do in the dark? Survival, he told himself. The essence of how to survive in a strange society is to learn all you can about the various customs and rituals and to get what help is available. Malvern could provide such help and, from the look of him, he would be willing to sell it.

"All right," said Kevin. "How much?"

"Now you're talking sense. "Two of us working together can do what one can't. We go in, grab the girl and split the bonus. Right?"

"Wrong," said Kevin.

"Sixty-forty? No? A straight third?" Malvern sighed. "You're a hard man," he said. "But you've got me at a disadvantage. "I'll tell you what—you foot all the bills and give me a flat quarter of the main take. A fifth, then," he snapped as Kevin shook his head. "That's my last word. A lousy twenty percent. Call it a deal and we can get started."

Kevin frowned. "How?" he demanded. "You're in jail."

"That's right," agreed Malvern. "So I am. Well, you'll just have to get me out, won't you?"

"How?"

"That's your problem." Malvern relaxed on the cot. "Now how about getting that bottle—partner?"

* * * *

Sig Shabalan, leading advocate of the world of Illagesh, leaned back in his chair and said: "Mr Blake, I admire you. You are a being of great determination. It is an attribute I have often noted among Terrestrials and it has undoubtedly something to do with the tremendous influence they have on all manner of cultures. You may have noticed many facets of the city which carry a sense of familiarity and now you know the cause. You can appreciate what I say. Would you like some tisane?"

"Thank you," said Kevin. "If you please."

"Not if I please, Mr Blake," said the advocate gently. "I realise that you are being polite but that is because I am both a travelled and a tolerant man. On this world such an expression immediately denigrates you to a servile capacity. You will drink only at my pleasure. That is hardly the attitude of a being which considers itself equal to its host. Would you like some tisane?"

"Yes," said Kevin. "Very much."

Beaming his appreciation at the correction Shabalan rang a bell. A girl entered the office with a tinkle of bells and a tray bearing cups and a steaming pot. Silently she placed it on the desk and withdrew.

"You will have noted that our menial classes, the servants and labourers and those of restricted intelligence are somewhat taciturn," said the advocate pouring the brew. "This is because they do not trust their ability to control their speech especially under the stimulus of high emotion. Your race does not appear to follow that procedure. Am I correct in my assumption?"

"You are." Kevin reached forward and took the proffered cup. It was of transparent porcelain bearing a motif of squares and circles in brilliant colour. "In fact the reverse is usually true."

"Which is why your client is in such a parlous situation. I must confess, Mr Blake, that I would not care to defend a client on such a serious charge in a Terrestrial court. You are a being of great courage and must have a great faith in your ability. Undoubtedly, on your own world, you rank high in your profession."

Which, thought Kevin bleakly, was not what the advocate thought it was. The facile lie he had invented had recoiled with boomerang-like effect. Finch must have talked and the word had got around. Going to Shabalan he had been met with a firm refusal to take Malvern's case coupled with a gracious offer of assistance to teach him the basics of the Illagesh legal system.

"More tisane?" Shabalan lifted the pot. "It is a special blend which tends to clear the mind and sharpen the facilities. I hesitate to suggest that a being of your capabilities needs such aids but your opponents have briefed a fine legal mind to act on their behalf. I would have taken the case myself but I do not wish to create bad feeling with our Terrestrial friends."

Glumly Kevin held out his cup for replenishing. "I feel that you do not think I have a chance of winning."

"To be frank, I do not." Scented steam drifted about the advocate's face as he lifted the pot. "Which is why no other advocate would accept the case after I had refused. And which is why," he added, "your client is so fortunate that you happened to be visiting our world at this time. A pity that you could not make a compromise but with such a perfect case I am not surprised the plaintiffs refused." He glanced at an ornamented wall-clock as a bell chimed. "Ah, it is time to leave for court. I shall watch you with great interest from the gallery."

The court was a box with seats for the advocates, the judge, the officials and waiting plaintiffs and those held for trial. The dock was wired to a lie-detector which dispensed with the need for a jury. Even though he was on a civil charge Malvern was treated exactly like the rest. He gave Kevin a weak smile as he was led into court.

"Hi!" he greeted. "Have you got all guns loaded and ready to fire?"

"I've no ammunition," said Kevin bleakly. "Are you certain you've told me the exact truth?"

"Yes."

"Are you positive? I've been studying this crazy system and we've only one chance. If you've lied I'm sunk."

"I've told you all I can," said Malvern. "It was dark, I was in a hell of a state, how can I be expected to remember every detail? All I know is that—" He broke off as an usher hissed for silence. "Remember the girl," he whispered. "And that bonus. Without me you don't stand a chance."

"Case 9765201," said the usher with a glare in their direction. "Dale Malvern, a Terrestrial, versus Halp Kreen and Qelk Ulgar, natives of Illagesh. Malvern defending. The case is one of determination of oral contract, your Honour. Jih Genarashal representing the plaintiff. Kevin Blake the defendant."

"A Terrestrial, I understand?"

"Yes, your Honour."

"Interesting. Will both advocates please step to the bench." From his lofty height the judge stared down at Kevin and his opponent. "On the face of it this is a simple matter," he said. "But in my experience few case of this kind are as simple as they appear. However, I must ask you both if there is any possibility of a mutually satisfactory compromise."

"No, your Honour," said Genarashal.

"In that case we must continue. Mr Blake, Sig Shabalan informs me that you are an accredited member of your profession. He also informs me that you are aware of the workings of our legal system. It seems most unlikely to me that you have been able to grasp more than a superficial knowledge in the short time you have been with us. Are you convinced in your own mind that you will be able to do full justice to your client?"

"I am, your Honour."

"It is to be hoped so. Very well, let the hearing commence."

Generashal cleared his throat. "The case for the plaintiffs is a simple one, your Honour, and rests on the wording of an oral contract made by the defendant during a journey from the Blue Hills. I quote, 'If there is anything I can do for you just let me know.' End of quote."

Kevin sucked in his breath. "I wish to challenge the exact wording, your Honour. Will the plaintiffs accept the sworn testimony of my client?"

"They have no choice, Mr Blake," said the judge drily. "You wish to place your client in the dock?"

"Yes, your Honour."

"Unless your defence is that the words were never uttered then I fail to see the point. However, if you insist—" He gestured to the usher. "Let the defendant enter the dock."

"All right," said Kevin softly to Malvern as, hands clamped on the electrodes, he glared at the judge. "Now whatever you do don't lie." In a louder voice he said; "Will you please tell the court of the events leading to the words you are stated to have uttered."

"It was dark," said Malvern, a green light flashing as to the truth of his words. "We were on our way back from the Blue Hills. I had two guides with me, the plaintiffs. We'd been travelling hard and I guess I got a little careless. I stepped into a patch of bog and would have gone under if they hadn't dragged me out. When they did I said: 'Thanks, you guys. If there's anything you want just ask'."

The light flashed red.

"You damned fool!" snapped Kevin. "Try again and get it right." To the judge he said; "I ask the tolerance of the court. My client was in a highly emotional state and it is natural that he could not remember his exact wording. However, for the purpose of the defence, they are important."

"As there is no denial of an oral contract and as you seem to regard the exact wording as important and as you are guest at our bar this court is inclined to be lenient," said the judge. "Proceed."

Sweating Malvern gripped the electrodes. "You've got to realise how it was," he blurted. "I was in mud up to my ears and for a minute there I thought they'd never get me out. When they did I just flopped. I was grateful and I said so. Hell, they'd just saved my life." He took a deep breath. "I guess I said 'Thanks a million. If ever there is anything I can do for you guys just let me know'."

Kevin released his breath as the light flashed green.

"An undeniable oral contract, your Honour, said Generashal with satisfaction. "However the defendant refuses to implement it which is why we are in court today. Halp Kreen has asked for a house and enough land to support himself and his family. Quelk Ulgar has asked for a fishing vessel. They are reasonable requests but neither has been met. Neither has any promise been made that they will be met. I rest my case."

The judge looked at Kevin. "The advocate for the defence may now address the court."

"I want an adjournment," blurted Kevin. "Ten minutes, your Honour. Please."

"For what reason?"

"To sturdy the financial implications of the claim made by the plaintiffs, your Honour. I assure you that it is relevant."

* * * *

It was borrowed time and he knew it but every little helped. Brooding over a pot of tisane he plotted his strategy. The judge was annoyed and would be biased, well, to hell with him. As far as he was concerned this would be his first and last appearance in any court. Especially as an advocate. Words, he thought. On Illagesh they were taken literally all the time. Malvern hadn't meant what he'd said, of course, but that was no defence at all. To survive in this situation you had to use their own rules. His one chance, that Malvern hadn't said what had been claimed, had vanished. Now he had to fall back on the reserves.

Back in court he cleared his throat and said: "Your Honour, I am not going to talk of the special circumstances in which the oral contract was made. I do not intend to plead that a man, a member of an emotional race, just rescued from a terrible form of death and not in full possession of his faculties should be forgiven for being a little too effusive with his praise and gratitude. Neither am I going to mention the fact that my client is a comparatively recent arrival to this world and not fully conversant with local legalities. Ignorance of the law, your Honour, is no excuse."

"I'm glad to hear you say it, Mr Blake," said the judge drily. "Do you intend to tell the court further details of what you do not intend to mention?"

"No, your Honour. I shall confine myself to the actual wording of the contract. I do not intend to mention the undoubted greed of the plaintiffs and their aggressive refusal to come to any compromise. Nor will I touch on the fact that truly civilised beings do not expect a reward for saving the life of a fellow creature. I—"

"Mr Blake!"

"—will keep strictly to the contract itself," continued Kevin ignoring the judge's frown. "Now what is a contract? I submit that to be valid in any legal sense a contract must contain at least two implications; the ability to perform the desire to receive. As an example may I propose an hypothetical situation in which an oysterman of Conch, in the heat of fevered passion, tells a local girl that he will give her ten thousand sons. Under Illagesh law that would be an oral contract. My submission is that it would be an invalid one on the grounds that not only could the promise not be fulfilled but the girl, the plaintiff in this case, would not want it to be fulfilled. She would be physically incapable of bearing such a number of sons. Do I make my point clear?"

"Are you making one, Mr Blake?" asked the heavily. "If so it eludes me. I suggest you keep to the point."

"I am, your Honour."

"Then continue."

"Thank you, your Honour." Kevin inflated his chest. "If such a contract in the circumstances which I have proposed is invalid then it follows that others of a similar nature must also lack legal sanction. Those spoken in extremes of emotional disturbance, for example. A creature stimulated beyond his normal emotional capacity can hardly be regarded as being in full possession of his normal faculties. In law no contract made by such a being can be regarded as binding."

"Are you claiming that your client is insane?" asked the judge ominously. "If so why were medical depositions not laid before this court prior to this hearing? Need I remind you of the penalties attending such infraction of the rules?"

"No, your Honour," said Kevin hastily. "It was just that—"

"For God's sake watch what you're doing!" Malvern interrupted. "Don't you know what they do with nuts on this planet?"

"Silence in court!" yelled an usher.

"I'm not crazy!" shouted Malvern.

"Shut up!" snapped Kevin. "I'm handling this!"

The judge slammed down his gavel. "Mr Blake, this court has been more than lenient but I warn you my patience is exhausted. You will keep to the point or I will have you arraigned for malpractice. You do your client no good by such conduct. Indeed, as an advocate, you leave much to be desired. The law is a dignified profession and we who practice it must maintain that dignity. Do I make myself clear?"

Damned clear, thought Kevin. So much for all the courtroom dramas he had watched on television back home. He sensed that he was on thin ice. A step wrong and they would start asking awkward questions. He didn't know what the penalties were for false misrepresentation and he didn't want to find out.

Humbly he said; "I am sorry, your Honour. I apologise if I have unwittingly offended the court."

"Your apology is accepted," said the judge, mollified. "Now please continue."

"The words of the contract," said Kevin, plunging straight to the heart of the matter. He quoted, "'If ever there is anything I can do for you guys just let me know.' I submit that the operative word in that contract is the word 'can'. It more than implies a restriction of the offer, it confines it to a certain, well-defined area, that of ability-to-produce. My client does not deny that a contract was uttered. He does not refuse to implement it. He simply refuses to perform the impossible."

Generashal lunged forward. "Your Honour, I protest! My colleague is being irrelevant, inept and inane. I—"

"Are you saying that I am talking a load of nonsense?" snapped Kevin.

"Your words are without meaning. You—"

"Your wife is ugly," said Kevin quickly. "Your mother was a harlot. Your children illegitimate. You are a disgusting sight to all normal persons."

"What!" Shocked, incredulous, Generashal spun to face his fellow advocate. "You dare to say such things! I'll—" He clapped his hand to his mouth.

"My words are meaningless," said Kevin blandly, admiring the other's self-control. "You said so yourself. So how can you take offence at such empty phrases? Of course your wife is not ugly, your mother was not a harlot, your children are not illegitimate and you are not a disgusting sight to all normal persons. Words are not without meaning, and it is foolish to say they are. The Illagesh culture is founded on the literal meaning of words. Your Honour, may I continue?"

"Well," said the judge, shaken. "I have never in all my experience ever witnessed such— But never mind. Continue."

"If ever there is anything I can do for you guys just let me know," said Kevin. "The actual words of my client which we do not dispute. Can, your Honour. Can!"

"So?"

"A man cannot do what it is beyond his ability to perform. The word, in such a context, means 'I will do what I am able'. My client is not able to provide a house and land sufficient to support a family. Neither is he able to provide a fishing vessel. He is devoid of funds, has no employment or hidden assets, and is quite simply unable to meet the demands of the plaintiffs."

"Your Honour!" Generashal stepped towards the bench.

"A moment." The judge lifted a thick tome and thumbed the pages. "You have a point, Mr Blake. I must agree that the use of the word 'can' did limit the execution of the contract."

"Even so, your Honour," said Generashal quickly. "It does not invalidate it. The implication still remains that the defendant will do everything in his power to meet any request. If he cannot, at present, provide the items desired then he can work to obtain them either in whole or in part."

"Not so, your Honour," said Kevin flatly. "The word not only implies the ability to perform but also the ability to perform at the particular time of the request. The request was made and my client did all he could. The contract was thus executed. The fact that my client was unable to meet the requests does not alter the fact in law."

"Now wait a minute!" said Generashal. "Are you saying that there is no case to answer?"

"I am." Kevin was firm. "In fact I submit that my client has been wrongfully detained."

"Logically you have a point, Mr Blake," said the judge. "But you would be charitable not to press it." His gavel slammed against its block. "The court finds for the defendant. He is relieved of all further responsibility for the contractual agreement and leaves this place without a stain on his character."

"You've done it! By God, you pulled it off!" Malvern dabbed at his sweating face. "Now let's get out of here. I need a drink."

"And Crystal Tarvainen," reminded Kevin.

"Sure. Just as soon as I can get the equipment," promised Malvern. "But first let's have that drink."

CHAPTER 6

An insect hummed, circled with a shimmer of wings and settled to feed. Kevin swore, slapped at his cheek, slapped again as the insect, unharmed, winged on its way. Watching it he tripped and fell into a bush, vicious thorns ripping at pants and blouse. One caught his hand leaving a thin trail of blood. Another clawed at his scalp. Carefully he pulled it free and climbed to his feet.

"I've told you before about watching your feet," said Malvern from one side of the bush. "That could have been a patch of bog or something with teeth. Quit worrying about a few flies."

"They bite," said Kevin.

Malvern shrugged. "So they bite. What did you expect? I warned you that it would be rough."

Which was a classic understatement, thought Kevin. For a week they had been climbing, pressing deeper into the Blue Hills, pushing through tangled underbrush and between endless trees. The straps of his pack dug into his shoulders, at night he rolled miserably on the hard ground, all the time he was uneasily aware of being totally at a loss in this primitive environment. Enviously he looked at the guides. The four natives waited patiently just ahead, completely at ease. They're in their element, he told himself. At home. But on Earth they'd be just as helpless as I am right now. It was no consolation. They weren't on Earth.

"You ready to move?" Malvern dug into a pocket of his loose jacket and produced a bottle. He sucked at it before holding it out. "Drink?"

Kevin shook his head.

"You should," urged his partner. "It comes out in the sweat and keeps the insects away. No? Well, just as you like." He sucked again and put the bottle back into his pocket. "Let's get moving."

Grimly Kevin plodded after the guides. All of them were armed with knives, machetes and rifles, missile weapons hard to damage and easy to use. The machetes were useful for cutting a path, the knives for whittling kindling for the night-time fires. He hoped they would never have to use the rifles. For hours they moved steadily onwards while the sun moved slowly towards the horizon. When the shadows began to press close Malvern called a halt.

"We'll camp here," he said. "Start clearing a space while I take a look ahead." He vanished into the gloom, his gross bulk soundless as he pressed between the bushes.

An expert, thought Kevin. A man who has learned to survive, and he wondered if he would be as good given time. But there was no need for that. He didn't intend living Malvern's kind of life. He was just going to find the girl, have a talk and persuade her to return. With the money he would take a nice, long vacation. Even if she didn't return he would dream up some story to satisfy Tarvainen. Ask for money to continue the quest, perhaps. Move from world to world, always staying in the cities, inventing a series of adventures.

Dropping his pack he joined the guides, swinging the machete and feeling the soreness of strengthening muscles. A space cleared he lit a fire and sat down, his back resting against a tree, dreaming as he looked into the flames.

The trial had been satisfactory. Shabalan had congratulated him and had hinted of the possibilities of a partnership if certain details could be arranged. Even Generashal had been generous enough to offer praise. Nice people, thought Kevin. Decent, clean, civilised. The girls were good looking too. Perhaps he should marry one and settle down. Illagesh was a pleasant world aside from the forests and he could stay away from those. A place by the sea, perhaps. His own beach. Unlimited sun and water, clean air, no sharing. Paradise!

"You damned fool!" Malvern came running towards him machete in hand. The bright blade swept back and descended with a thud three inches above his head. Something fell on his shoulder and twitched on the ground.

"A viner," said Malvern as Kevin jumped to his feet. "Didn't I warn you about them? Put weight against the trunk and the vine comes down to eat. Once it gets a grip you'll never get loose. You'd have to cut it away and it leaves a nasty wound." He kicked at the rope-like strand. "Where are the boys?"

Kevin looked around but failed to see the guides.

"Probably collecting some dainties," said Malvern. "This far up in the hills you get a centipede they're fond of. Or maybe they don't want to get too close to the fire."

"Why not?"

"It could attract things." Malvern laughed at his partner's expression. "Don't worry, I'm here to protect you. How about getting something to eat?"

They ate from cans and packets, using water from canteens. The fire died to a dull glow and the guides returned, sitting like statues in the surrounding darkness. A thin breeze rustled the tops of the trees and, high above, visible through the branches, stars shone with a remote beauty.

"You know," said Malvern thoughtfully. "I've been thinking. Twenty percent isn't very much. Not when you consider that you don't stand a chance without me."

"We made a deal," said Kevin shortly.

"Deals can be changed."

"Not this one. How much longer do we have to travel?"

"Not too far now." Malvern stretched and produced his bottle. "Of course, without me to guide you, you could wander around for a year without finding her. That's if you managed to stay alive that long. On the other hand I guess I owe you something for getting me out of jail. You ever met her?"

"Crystal Tarvainen? No."

"A real kook," said Malvern. He sucked at his bottle and spat into the fire. Flames reared to paint his mottled face red and yellow. "Nowhere but Earth could breed women like that. A spoiled, stupid, sadistic bitch. Rich, too, that makes it worse. Why do the wrong people always have the money?"

"I don't know," said Kevin. It was a question he'd often asked himself. "Fate, I guess. Or just plain luck. Tell me about the girl."

"She's crazy," said Malvern. "On top of everything else she's crazy. She has to be. Would a normal girl with her kind of money do the things she does?"

"They might given the chance," said Kevin. "But stick to the point."

"The point," grinned Malvern. "Remember that judge? Hell, for a minute I thought he was going to throw the book at you. And the way you spoke to that advocate! If you hadn't covered up you could have been in real trouble. He could have sued you for everything you owned grounds of broadcast slander. You were lucky."

"It was a calculated risk," said Kevin. "The girl?"

"Crystal Tarvainen," said Malvern. "When she arrived here she heard about the nomads in the Blue Hills and had to see what they were like. So what does she do? She goes out to find them and she's with them now. Or was when I saw her. I managed to reach their lower camp with a load of knives and tried to buy her from the chief. He wouldn't sell. Then I managed to get in touch with her and she didn't want to leave. I had guides waiting beyond the camp and it would have been simple to sneak away in the dark but would she, hell. Said there were things she had to finish, that she was free and of age, and why didn't I mind my own damn business?"

"True enough," said Kevin.

Malvern shrugged. "Maybe, but what's that got to do with it? Anyway, she finally made me a proposition. I was to gamble with her. If I won she'd give me a draft on her account. If I lost—" He broke off, shuddering. "I lost. The next thing I know is she was yelling fit to split my eardrums and the whole tribe came running. They put me in a cage and left me hanging for the night. I had the idea they intended to do something with me at dawn and whatever it was I figured I could do without it. One of the bars was weak and I managed to escape just before the sun rose. I found my guides and we all got the hell away while the going was good. The rest you know."

"The game she made you play," said Kevin thoughtfully. "What was it?"

Malvern lowered his bottle. "Does it make any difference?"

"It might. What was it?"

"Dice," said Malvern. "We rolled highest number for first throw. I had to hit a seven before she did. I didn't make it."

A game of chance, pondered Kevin, or so it would appear to a simple mind, but could it have been more than that? The girl could have been afraid, a terrified prisoner longing for someone to rescue her. An apparent trader had appeared but did he possess the strength and luck necessary to succeed? Had he won the contest she may, obeying the dictates of fate, have agreed to have returned with him. The draft could simply have been a means to make him cooperate. Or had she been performing some esoteric ritual dictated by the customs of the tribe?

Musing he leaned against his pack looking at the red glow of the fire. How would a young and tender girl, the product of a highly technological civilisation, manage to survive in a primitive culture? Become a priestess? Claim supernatural powers? Use her superior knowledge to aid and guide her new friends? Marry the strongest man around? For some reason the thought was offensive.

"Malvern," he said. "When you saw her was she with anyone?"

"Uh?"

"Did she have a husband or a protector or something?"

"That girl needs protection like I need a hole in the head," said Malvern thickly. "Now pipe down and get some rest."

"I need facts," said Kevin. "Data to work on. Tell me what you noticed about the camp."

Malvern grunted, not answering, already asleep. Well, thought Kevin, it didn't matter. He would begin probing tomorrow. When he was alert and his mind fresh to tackle the problem. It couldn't be as hard as Malvern had made out. He had probably entirely misunderstood the situation.

Yawning Kevin settled down to sleep. When he woke it was day. The fire was dead. The guides had vanished and the bright point of a spear was hovering three inches above his throat.

It was held by a five-foot frog neatly dressed in tunic, pants and boots of scaled leather ornamented with abstract designs. A crested helmet covered the domed skull, the long visor shielding the goggling eyes. The wide mouth gave it the appearance of smiling but there was nothing funny about the spear. Kevin recoiled from it, eyes on the wickedly sharp blade.

"Ah," said the frog. "So you are alive. I was beginning to doubt."

"I'm alive." Kevin retreated further and climbed to his feet. Malvern was nowhere to be seen. "Do you mind lowering that spear?"

"Of course, my dear fellow. A neat device, is it not? Collapsible shaft for easy portability, weighted butt and non-corrosive metal for blade and stem. Useful, too." The spear slammed into the dirt a foot from where Kevin stood. Impaled, a multi-legged creature gnashed at the steel. "Ugly thing, is it not?" boomed the frog and casually flipped the dying insect into the ashes of the fire.

"Thanks," said Kevin.

"Think nothing of it. We intelligent beings must stick together. How many were in your party?"

"Two. We had four guides."

"The guides have departed," said the frog. "They most probably sensed our coming and took evasive action. Your friend, unfortunately, is dead."

"Dead?"

"Regrettably so. We found him while searching the vicinity of your camp." The frog gestured to where others of his kind moved among the surrounding bushes. "Do you wish to see him? No? Well each race to their customs."

"How did he die?" demanded Kevin.

The frog shrugged. "He could have departed in many ways. He could have swallowed some poisonous substance. He could have reached the end of his natural term. He could have been attacked by some venomous creature. In point of fact his head had been severed by some sharp instrument. I suspect the guides. They must have intended to kill and rob you both. As it happened our coming most probably saved your life. I trust that you are grateful?"

"Most grateful," said Kevin. "If there is anything I can do—"

"There is." The frog slapped Kevin's pockets with his free hand, deftly removing all items of value. "Is this all the money you have?"

"Yes."

"It isn't much. Are you sure?"

"I've had expenses," said Kevin tightly. "Expeditions don't come cheap on Illagesh. What you have there is all I own."

"Too bad," said the frog.

It was more than that. Despite Ransom's efforts Tarvainen hadn't been all that generous, or maybe the agent had taken too large a slice of the cake. The money represented his travelling expenses back to Earth. Without it he would be stranded.

"My dear, fellow," said the frog blandly when Kevin pointed out the facts. "You really amaze me. You could honestly admit that we have saved your life and yet you fret about a little money. Suppose you had been killed, would money have helped you then? Of course not. Life, surely, must be worth all you possess for without life what are possessions. I will go further. As we have saved your life it now, morally, belongs to us. The logic is inescapably as I'm sure you will agree."

"Now wait a minute," said Kevin anxiously. "I—"

"Waiting is not possible," interrupted the frog. "Time, as they say, is money. Do you wish to conduct any rites over your friend? Eat his heart, perhaps? Remove a portion of his anatomy for a keepsake? The head, in its present condition, is quite portable. I could supply the loan of a container if you wish."

Kevin shuddered. Malvern alive was one thing. Malvern dead was another. He had never seen a dead person and had no desire to break the record.

"Think about it," urged the frog. "I would not like to offend the customs of any intelligent creature. No? Well, let us be on our way."

Kevin stood his ground. "Where to?"

"That you will see when we get there." The spear lifted, the point touching the skin just below Kevin's chin. Gently it pressed. "I would be most reluctant to cause you physical discomfort," said the frog. But as we have agreed that, logically, your life now belongs to us you cannot blame me or safeguarding our property. Also," it added, "I doubt if you would survive for long in this wilderness without our protection. Shall we proceed?"

Having no choice Kevin obeyed, climbing higher into the Blue Hills with his new-found friends. There were six of them, two bounding along in the front, two at the rear and one at either side. His captor's name, he discovered, was Kvoom, and he was loquacious.

"Nice," it said as its long, thin tongue flashed out to snare a passing insect. "Many of these primitive worlds have great advantages. Lunch on the wing, so to speak. Most convenient."

Kevin rubbed his stomach. It was close to noon and he was getting hungry. "When do we eat?"

"All the time," said Kvoom. He caught another insect, chewed and swallowed. "See?"

"Real food," said Kevin desperately. "I'm starving."

"Hunger is an attitude of mind," said the frog loftily. "Think of other things and the desire for food will cease to bother you. How can a man feel carnal needs when he gazes on the beauty of a stagnant pool?"

"A philosopher," sneered Kevin.

"A poet," corrected the frog. "If you wish I will beguile you with one of my compositions. Baroom," it chanted without waiting for Kevin to reply, "karoom, ting. Shoom, thoom, ping. Ahluss, maruss, zing. I call it The Effusive Sounds of Stricken Metal On Symana On A Warm Afternoon," it continued cheerfully. "Friends have told me that they have actually heard the delicate chime of temple bells echoing from over the water. Did you manage to hear them?"

"Well—"

"You have to concentrate, naturally, and this is hardly the most appropriate setting. You would like another?"

"Shut up, Kvoom," boomed the frog on Kevin's other side. "You want to tell everyone we're here?"

"A peasant," said Kvoom softly, coming closer to Kevin's side as he followed the trail left by the creatures leading the way. "Undoubtedly the product of contaminated spawn. But there it is. A man cannot always choose his companions. You have artistic abilities yourself, perhaps?"

"Yes," said Kevin. "I write."

"Poetry?"

"Prose, though I have composed a few poems," he added quickly. "Simple little things hardly worth your attention and I would never presume to recite them now that I have heard The Effusive Sounds Of Stricken Metal On Symana On A Warm Afternoon. A true work of natural genius overriding the barriers of race and creed."

Kvoom beamed. "You really think so?"

"For many years I was the art critic on one of our mediums of mass communication," lied Kevin. "It was my duty to select works of merit for a discerning audience. Had I had the good fortune to have seen your poem I would have blazoned it in letters of fire for all to see. May I hear it again?"

The flanking guard snarled as Kvoom lifted its voice. "By the Original Egg, can't you keep quiet? It's bad enough in camp without you making that racket now!" Savagely it thrust at a bush with its spear. "Damned intellectuals." It muttered. "Crazy, the lot of them."

"You're stunted," said Kvoom. "Emotionally scarred. You can't appreciate the finer things of life."

"There's nothing wrong with me," grunted the frog. Again its spear stabbed at a bush. Something shrilled and darted across the path. "Just give me a nice, warm, stagnant pool and I'm happy. I don't tear myself apart wanting what I can't get. And I don't upset those I have to work with by acting the fool," it said pointedly. "Keep it up and I'll complain to the captain."

"Who's he?" asked Kevin.

"A hard man," snapped the frog. "Now keep quiet or we'll tie you up and sling you from a pole."

* * * *

The rest of the day passed in silence, labour and mounting discomfort. At dusk Kevin saw a glimmer of light ahead which grew into a roaring fire as they reached the camp. Another dozen frogs stood about, some busy over piled bales, others resting. A tent stood to one side the flaps open, a table and chair visible through the parted fabric. A big frog sat at the table, its crested helmet adorned with brilliant plumes.

"What's this?" it snapped. "You lads were supposed to be out collecting skins not looking for guests." It quietened a little as Kvoom explained. "So this creature owes us its life, eh? Well, that's different. Take a seat, my dear fellow. Hungry? Kvoom, get some food."

Gratefully Kevin accepted the something fried on a stick which the poet collected from the fire. It had crisped wings and scales together with a multitude of legs but he brushed them off and sank his teeth into the roasted flesh. It was surprisingly succulent, a local dainty, he imagined, and he concentrated on getting it down.

"Feel better?" The captain reached for a jug. "A little something to wash it down?"

"Please." Kevin swallowed what seemed to be a mixture of fly-juice and grit. Gagging he set down the cup. "That was nice but have you any water?"

"Anything you want, my dear fellow," boomed the captain. A nice, long draught of tepid water is just the thing after a long day's march." It reached for another jug. "Tell me, it said confidentially. "Did you have anything of value in your camp? Skins or gems, perhaps? Rare bones or feathers? No? Are you positive?"

"Nothing," said Kevin. "We weren't hunting. Anyway, the guides stole all we possessed. With the exception of my money," he added, remembering. "Kvoom took that."

"I see." The captain drummed webbed fingers on the table. "You can't trust them," it explained. "They go out and maybe they work and maybe they don't. If they'd found anything valuable at your camp they could have hidden it or failed to report it. I have to be on their backs all the time."

"The money," said Kevin. "Can I have it back, please?"

"Well, now," said the captain. "I'm afraid not. It comes under the heading of legitimate spoils and will be used to off-set the cost of this expedition. What are you?"

Kevin blinked. "A man."

"I mean what do you do? What is your profession?"

"I write."

"A writer," mused the frog. "Not much call for them at the moment. In fact I can't remember when last there was a demand. Can't you do anything else? Hunt? Farm? Play a musical instrument?"

"I used to be a clerk at the Transworld Trading Company."

The captain beamed. "That's better. A scribe, eh. Anything else?"

"I was an advocate for a short while. Won all my cases too."

"Better still. How about manual work? No? Well, I guess we'll have to make the most of what we've got." Reaching for a form the captain scribbled in appropriate sections and passed it over. "Just sign that and you can get some rest."

Cautiously Kevin looked at the document. "What is it?"

"A standard indenture form. Just sign in the place I've marked."

"Not so fast," said Kevin, and carefully read the printed form. It stated that for certain benefits received the undersigned agreed to work for the owner of the contract at any task the said owner should determine as long as the labour was in the field of clerical work, writing, speaking, serving, manipulation and adjustment for a period of ten years from the present date.

Firmly he put it down. "I'm not signing that."

"Why not?" The captain was puzzled. "Something wrong?"

"It mentions certain benefits I've received. What benefits?"

"The use of my men to guide you to safety. Food and drink on arrival. Be a good fellow, now. Sign and let us get this tedious business over."

"No," said Kevin. "What the hell is this, anyway? Slavery is illegal. If I sign that that's just what I'd be for the next ten years. I won't do it."

The captain glowered, his throat pulsing ominously.

"Are you going to be unreasonable about this? Must I remind you that you owe us your life? Morally I have the right to sell your services for the remainder of your natural span, but I am not a man like that. All we ask is a short ten years. It could have been twenty. But greed is not a vice of my race. Sign now like a decent creature, have a drink and let us forget this unpleasant moment."

"And if I don't?"

"Kvoom!" roared the captain. "Put this thing in cage!"

It was six feet tall, three feet a side, large enough for a frog and probably used to enforce discipline, but Kevin was no frog. He couldn't stand, sit or lie with any real degree of comfort. The only tolerable position was to squat cross-legged with his back rammed hard against the bars. He tried it for a while and then, with both legs feeling as if they had been set on fire, decided that the captain wasn't to change its mind and let him out.

Painfully he rose and examined his prison. The bar were of thick wood lashed with wire. The door was held by a padlock and chain, the hinges of rustless metal fastened with deeply-sunk screws. Resting his stooped shoulders against the roof Kevin strained with all the force of back and legs. Nothing moved. Taking a deep breath he tried again, sparks flashing before his eyes, and then squatted down again in order to think.

He was, he decided, in a hell of a mess. Without money he couldn't leave the planet even if he managed to find his way back to the spaceport and he didn't think he could even do that. If he signed the indenture he could kiss freedom goodbye for a decade and probably longer. And if he didn't sign it the captain would keep him in the cage, probably without food or water, until he either died or gave in.

Well, suppose he did sign? No civilised world recognised the validity of a contract signed under duress. Certainly not the Illagesh legal system. He could sign and then, when they reached town, complain. Shabalan would help him, maybe, or Generashal. Finch certainly, he'd gained the impression that the factor had no great love of aliens. He might even be able to get his money back.

Impulsively he rattled the bars of the cage.

"Knock it off," boomed a voice. "You want to wake up the entire camp?" A figure loomed against the dying lights of the fire and a guard, armed with a spear, came forward to peer into the cage. Kvoom? The hope died as the frog came closer. It was an older creature with a hooded eye and warted skin. "Something biting you?"

"I'm thirsty."

"Too bad."

"Wait a minute," said Kevin as the frog turned to go. "I'm lonely. Let's talk."

The frog sighed and stuck the point of his spear into the dirt. "You people! Yak, yak, yak all the time. You're as bad as Kvoom. That creep'll clot the spawn on a lily. What do you want to know?"

"When are you pulling out from here?"

"Why ask me? I'm not the captain."

"Listen," said Kevin urgently as the frog reached for its spear. "Don't go yet. Would you like to make some private money?"

"How much?"

"A lot. You'll get it when we reach town. Finch will give it to you."

"Finch?"

"The factor. You must have seen him. An old guy, a Terrestrial. Everyone in town knows him. He's a friend of mine and will do as I say." He glared at the hooded eye. "What's the matter? Don't you believe me?"

"Sure I believe you," said the frog. "But what town are you talking about?"

"The one with the spaceport."

"Which spaceport? We came in at Lake Dengue and that's the way we'll be going back. It's away over the other side of the Blue Hills. There's no Finch there that I know of."

Bleakly Kevin stared after the retreating figure of the guard, cursing himself for not thinking of the obvious. Illagesh was a large planet. Naturally it would have more than one city and more than one spaceport. It just hadn't occurred to him.

He'd moved too fast, he decided. Been in too much of a hurry. Instead of quietly gathering information he'd rushed around like a mad thing. Getting involved with the local legal system in order to get Malvern out of jail. And where was Malvern now? Dead. A fine favour I did him, he thought. He could be safe in jail now instead of lying out in the forest. And what had he achieved? Nothing. As yet hadn't even seen his quarry and from the look of things he wasn't going to. Either he would die in the cage or be sold into virtual slavery.

Survival, he thought bitterly, squatting and trying to ignore the ache in his legs. It was one thing to write a book on how to do it, quite another to actually put what he'd written into practice. And yet it was all he had to work with. His mind, mouth and stolen information.

Gloomily he crushed a centipede gnawing at his boot.

CHAPTER 7

"I don't like this," said the frog captain. The spear lifted in its webbed hand, sunlight glinting from the point and edge of the wicked blade. "I don't like it at all."

Which makes two of us, thought Kevin. I don't like it either. Miserably he eased the crushing burden on his shoulders. In the cage it had seemed a neat way out of all his troubles. Simply win the cooperation of the frogs to find the nomads and then persuade the girl to buy his freedom. But there had been snags. One of them was that the captain had forced him to sign the indenture before agreeing to move. As insurance, it had explained, as something to fall back on should the venture fail. And the creature had increased the term from ten years to twenty. True, Kevin had insisted on a conditional quit-claim but it would be valueless if they didn't find the girl.

Another irritating thing was the way he had been treated. Like a mindless beast of burden, loaded with equipment, his hands chained. At first he had been sure the physical effort would kill him, but, as the days passed, he had managed to find some strength. Now the captain was becoming impatient.

"We've been looking too long," it grumbled, toying with the spear. "I don't like it. Where is this camp which you claim holds the woman?"

"I don't know." Kevin dabbed sweat from his streaming features. "I told you, Malvern was the one who knew just where to find her and he got himself killed. The guides could have helped but they've vanished. How about taking off these chains?"

"Why?"

"So that I can scratch my back," said Kevin. "It itches."

"Is that all? You don't intend to escape?"

"Where would I go?" Kevin looked at the surrounding underbrush and trees. "Anyway, I am a man of honour. I've given you my word. And if you don't treat me right the girl will be annoyed. It's bad enough having to carry your gear without being chained up like a prisoner."

"A man has the right to protect his property," said the captain. "You're mine for the next twenty years. And someone has to carry the gear so why not you? Do you expect me to do it?" Stepping back it glared up at the tree. "See anything?"

"I'm not sure," called a voice from above. "Maybe if I can get a little higher?" Leaves rustled from the topmost branches. "I think— Yes! Over to the north! I can just see a column of smoke."

"It's the camp," said Kevin thankfully. "It must be."

"Take a bearing!" boomed the captain to the invisible watcher and turned to Kevin. "This girl, you're positive that she's rich?"

"Her father owns half of Earth. She could buy all of Illagesh if she wished. You don't have to worry about getting your money. And she'll give you a reward," added Kevin. "This will be the most profitable expedition you've ever conducted. How about taking off these chains now?"

"Later, maybe." The captain stepped towards the tree down which a frog came sliding. "Did you get the bearing. "Is it far?"

Casually the creature brushed a mass of hooked and hungry leeches from his clothes and skin. "It wasn't bad up there," it beamed. "Plenty of good, fat flies. With a little effort a man could get along real well on this world."

"You disfigured product of poisoned spawn!" boomed the captain. "Make your report! Is it far?"

"Not far," said the frog, offended. "We should reach there by dusk. And I'll have you know that I came from a batch of the best spawn on—"

"Forget it!" The captain roared at the column. "Ready? March!"

Kevin fell into line with a dozen frogs all loaded with packs smaller than his own. The rest spread out to front and rear, the captain taking the lead. He moved fast but Kevin didn't mind. The quicker they reached the camp the sooner his ordeal would be over. Find the girl and have a few words and his chains and pack would fall from his aching body. A few more and the indenture would go up in smoke. Then a little persuasion and she would either accompany see him safely on his way back to civilised luxury.

She would be glad to see him, he decided, trotting under the weight of his pack. A clean, decent, civilised girl like that must be starved for company of her own kind. She would be eager to talk of the latest news from home, the latest television plays; books even. He would lift her mind from the undoubted squalor of the camp and the people around. I'll be like a breath of fresh wind, he told himself. Human, cultured, a reminder of what she has left and really needs.

The thought maintained him as they pressed on through the day. Twice they halted so as to get fresh bearings on the column of smoke and once they had to detour around a wide area splotched with bare soil beneath which lurked unpleasant forms of life.

"A phren-nest," explained Kvoom as they resumed their course. "Ugly things. Tread on or close to those patches of dirt and they'll have you. All legs and eyes and a horrible sting. They shove it in you and you can't blink an eye. Then they eat you, slowly."

"Nice," said Kevin bleakly. Alone he would have crossed the patch and been glad of the lack of underbrush.

"For the phren, maybe. Fresh meat for weeks. But not for the victim. Just think of it, my friend. Paralysed but conscious. Can you imagine the depth of pain and despair? The terrible loneliness, lying there in the dark, hearing the rustle of legs, knowing that you are being slowly devoured? What a magnificent theme for a poem! I must work on it immediately. Eek, ooh, aah," it mused thoughtfully. "Or should it be Aargh, ugh, nooo? Never mind, it will come."

"I'm sure it will," said Kevin. He swore as he stumbled and almost fell. It was growing dark, thick shadows hiding details, and his eyes ached from straining ahead to see the light of welcome fires.

"It is advisable to keep one's balance at all times," said Kvoom. "Especially when a carried burden raises one's centre of gravity."

"I'll try and remember that," gritted Kevin.

"Do. It may help. In fact Kvoom broke off as a yell came from the front of the column. "What is happening? It sounds as if we have met a difficulty. I must— Awk!" The frog collapsed one webbed hand clutching the feathered shaft which rose from its gizzard. Kevin dropped to his knees as something whistled through the space his head had occupied. The poet was dying. Weakly it rolled its dimming eyes. "The irony of fate," it wheezed. "My greatest work unfinished."

"Baroom, karoom, ting," said Kevin quickly. "Shoom, thoom, ping. Ahluss, maruss, zing. The author of those words will never be forgotten." It was all that he could do.

He ducked as a spear lanced from the shadows to stick quivering in the dirt. He heard the captain's booming roar. "To arms! We are attacked! Gather around me!"

The maddened frog came racing back down the trail as Kevin snatched at the knife in the dead poet's belt. If he could only cut free that damned pack! He didn't have a chance. Spear levelled, voice rising above the croaks dying, the captain charged in for the kill.

"You traitor!" it roared. "You foul and disgusting eater of spawn! You led us into a trap!"

To protest was useless. Kevin rose to his feet, sprang to one side as the spear lanced forward, fell as the weight of the pack jerked him off-balance. Helplessly he looked up at the vengeful captain, the spear gripped in both webbed hands.

"Die!" boomed the frog. "You filthy spoiler of water! Die!"

"No!" yelled Kevin. "Don't! I'm innocent!"

He cringed as the spear lifted for the killing thrust. A shadow rose behind the frog and smashed a club against the crested helmet. It fell from the sloping skull which collapsed into pulp beneath a second blow. A tall native wearing feathers, beads, paint and a loin cloth stepped over the body and looked at Kevin. Thoughtfully he lifted his club.

"No!" yelled Kevin again. He lifted his chained wrists. "I'm a man, a prisoner, see? Take me to your leader."

It was a hell of a journey. Still wearing the pack, ankles lashed together, he was slung on a pole and carried like a dead beast. Every step sent jolts of pain through limbs and ankles. Grimly he clung to the shaft which had been slipped through the chain in order to save his wrists. Before and behind his captors grunted beneath the weight of their booty.

It was thick dark by the time they reached the village. Kevin had a confused impression of tents, shacks made of leaves and bark, leaping fires which painted watching faces with shifting colours. A tent, larger than the rest, ugly with hideous designs stood at the far end of the settlement. His bearers trotted towards it, dropped their load and removed the pole. Writhing on the dirt Kevin sensed a general withdrawal, a sudden hush. Looking up he saw the flap of the tent drawn aside and a tall figure emerge to stand in the dancing firelight.

"Well, well," said a soft, caressing voice. "What have we here?"

Kevin grunted, fighting his anguish, determined to be cool.

"Good evening," he said. "Crystal Tarvainen, I presume?"

* * * *

She was tall and beautiful and lovelier than he had imagined from the photograph. Generous too, rested, fed, washed of the accumulated grime of his journeying, Kevin sat in a wood and thong chair and stared at his hostess. The hair, he decided, warm with the colour of trapped sunshine, was just about perfect. The skin of her naked arms and what he could see of her shoulders and legs was a delicately tanned velvet. She wore a simple dress ornamented with beads, caught at the waist with a pouched belt supporting a sheathed knife. Above and below her body swelled in tantalising femininity.

Rubbing his itching palms he said; "How did a nice girl like you get in a place like this?"

"I don't know," she said. "I guess I was just lucky."

"I mean it," Kevin insisted. "You're sweet, lovely, charming and attractive. Why hole yourself up in a stinking village with a bunch of nomads? What does it get you?

"When characters like you find me a pain in the rear."

"I'm serious."

"And so am I." She took a chair and sat facing him across a table of rough planks spiked to rougher legs. "Listen," she said. "I didn't ask you to come looking for me and I wish that you'd never arrived. The men must be getting soft, they should have disposed of you with the rest, but no, they had to dump you on my doorstep. Maybe you'll wish they hadn't."

With dignity he said: "I come bearing a message your father. He needs you."

"Like hell he does!"

"He's old," said Kevin. "Almost facing his end. He wants to see his little girl for perhaps the last time. How can you refuse?"

"Easily."

"But he's your father!"

Irritably she rose and began to pace the confines of the tent. It was a weird place hung with dried bones, gourds, various leaves and assorted spears and bows. A modern lasergun rested on a bracket. A curtain hung before a bed. Stainless metal travelling cases stood beside plastic boxes on the floor which was covered by a mess of skins. A doctor box supported an everlasting lamp. A dreamlight glowed with ever-changing colour. A tall cabinet of woven reeds held clothing.

"You're a damned nuisance," she said. "A prying nurd, but I'll try and explain. Dear Daddy doesn't give a damn about me and the feeling is mutual. I saw him maybe four times before I was ten and then once a year after that if I was lucky. All he cares about is making money. When mother died she left me her estate and now he's got itching fingers. He wants me to sign over certain properties so that he can start a new development. Once he gets me back on Earth he'll manage to nail me down some way until I agree to cooperate."

Kevin frowned. "That doesn't make sense," he protested. "You could do business through any planetary embassy."

"I know that."

"Then why not do it? Get him off your back? Or is he trying to rob you?"

"If he tried that I'd break his neck," she said coldly. "It's just that I'm not interested. I've got all the money I need and all I want is the freedom to enjoy it as I wish. Satisfied?"

He wasn't but knew better than to argue. A strange person, he decided. Wilful. And a little crazy too. How could anyone with all that money be content to wander around doing all the things she had? This tent, for example. It stank of primitiveness and he'd bet it had vermin in the cracks of the supports. Insects and maybe other things which would come out at night and scuttle around. No wonder she had a doctobox! Who could tell what foul disease a person might collect in such a place?

Well, he would rescue her no matter what. Not at once, of course, first he would win her confidence, gain her friendship and then, when the time was right, he'd move. On Earth they would be able to do something for her. Cure her of her obvious mental instability, perhaps. It was a pity that such a beautiful girl should be such a nut.

"What do you do?" she demanded. "Aside from chasing women, I mean."

"I write."

"Books?" She looked interested. "Do you ever get them published?"

"Naturally." He waved a negligent hand. "As a matter of fact my latest might be of interest to you. Survival in Society. I deal in depth of the manner in which a person can adapt himself to various circumstances and remain a master of any situation in which he may find himself."

"Is that so," she said, smiling. "A pity you didn't read it."

"I don't understand what you mean?"

"Well, you haven't done so good for yourself, have you?" she pointed out. "Almost killed in the forest, humped here like a lump of meat, wholly at my mercy. Call that surviving? It seems to me that I could teach you a thing or two about that. How else do you think I got where I am?"

"With money," he snapped irritably. "You probably bribed them to let you stay as a guest. Anyway, where is the boss around here? I asked to be taken to their leader."

"I am the leader."

Shocked, Kevin searched her face to see if she was lying He couldn't tell. But Malvern had told him that he had tried to buy her from the chief which had to mean that there was someone in greater authority. He had said other things too but had probably been exaggerating. Kevin decided not to mention his ex-partner. The knowledge he had gained he would use as his own.

"I'm talking about the real leader," he said. "The chief."

Her smile took on a touch of cynicism. "I am the chief, the other one lost out and I took his place. That's what I mean about survival, it was him or me. I'm still around and he's long gone."

"Dead?"

"Unless he can stand to be eaten, yes."

Kevin eased his collar. "You killed him?"

"Let's just say that he had served his period of usefulness. Primitives are like that, you know. They can't see any point in carrying dead weight. The chief was old and he flopped when it came to the crunch. So—" She drew a finger sharply across her throat. "Now I'm the new seer."

"Uh?"

"The prophet. The guider of destiny. The looker into the future. The bringer of game, the easer of anguish, the reader of the runes. Hell, you're a writer, don't you know what a seer is?"

"Of course I know," he snapped, offended. "It was a little unexpected, that's all. But aren't you scared? I mean, suppose someone does to you what you did to the old chief?"

This time she laughed outright, the clear notes sounding like bells. "Who? You? Brother, you wouldn't stand a chance! Now get out of here and let me change."

Sombrely Kevin wandered about the village. It was the mess he'd expected, piles of rubbish thick with flies, garbage and noisome messes lying between the tents and shacks. A typical nomad scene. When things grew too bad they would simply move to a new spot and start all over. With fruit and berries and game, food would be no problem. At times they probably traded at one of the cities but mostly they would keep well away from civilisation. Indians, he thought, and halted, thinking. The Great West and before. He'd done a book about them once. Tribes with strong cultures and customs. Frowning he tried to remember the information he'd gathered during long sessions in the library. Magic and mystery and fertility rites. Trials of strength and the penalties of failure.

Details were vague and he continued his perambulations. A group of children sat in a circle and threw coloured stones, gambling, he guessed, using seeds as tokens. It seemed to be the main village pastime, even the women sat chattering as they threw the primitive dice. The men seemed more concerned with spear-throwing and practice with bows and arrows.

One of them approached Kevin as he neared the butts.

"Care for a go, friend? Your boots against my best loin cloth. Best two out of three. Agreed?"

"No thanks," said Kevin.

"I'll give you odds," suggested a spear-thrower. "Two to one. If you get more than half my score you win. Your blouse against a bunch of feathers and my second wife."

Kevin shook his head.

"A couple of helmets, then? We got plenty from the frogs. Or how about a gallon of that stuff they drink? I can get it if you agree."

"Wait a minute," said Kevin thinking. "Did you strip the things you killed?"

"Sure, why not. No point in letting good meat go to waste." The native grinned at Kevin's expression. "You don't like roast frog? Well, every man to his taste."

"Their gear," said Kevin. "Their supplies. The captain's belt?"

"That stuff?" The native casually threw his spear dead centre of the target. "We handed all that stuff over to the boss."

Relieved Kevin hurried back to the big tent and ducked inside. Crystal yelled, grabbed at her knife and retreated, clutching something bright to her naked form.

"Get out of here!" she stormed. "Get out before I find out what you're like inside!"

Ignoring her Kevin searched the tent, finding what he was looking for under a heap of skins. Helmets, knives assorted belts. He dived into their pouches without success.

"Is this what you're looking for?" Crystal, now dressed in a shimmering gown patterned with abstract motifs held up a slip of paper. "An indenture," she said. "Signed by Kevin Blake. A twenty-year agreement."

"Conditional," he snapped. "I've got the quit-claim." He flung down the last of the belts. "Where is my money?"

"Your money?"

"Those damned frogs stole it from me. You must have it. It was in one of these belts, it had to be. I'd like it back if you don't mind."

* * * *

It was night, from somewhere in the village a drum was beating like a gigantic heart and the leaping glow of fires threw dancing shadows against the wall of his tent. Kevin stirred, felt a vicious bite at his neck and slammed his hand against something which squashed. Wearily he sat upright on the skins which formed his bed. Stinking things, full of vermin, hardly any protection against the hard ground. Around him men grunted and snored, scratching automatically at their naked skins.

Rising Kevin stepped over his tent-mates into the open. A bright light shone in the big tent which Crystal used and her silhouette showed sharp and clear against the wall. Kevin felt like ramming a spear directly into it.

A cow, he thought. A vicious, sadistic, unprincipled bitch! She hadn't returned the money. She hadn't agreed to loan him his fare. She had refused even his request for guides so that he could return to civilisation. Instead she had laughed.

Well, maybe he would be the one to have the final gloat.

But how? It wasn't going to be easy, he decided. At the moment she probably thought him a real nurd, an Earthsider still wet behind the ears, a useless idiot who hadn't learned the first basic lesson on how to get along. To command her respect and obedience he had to appear tougher than she was, more adaptable. But again, how? He was useless with weapons, couldn't find his way through the forest and was broke into the bargain. Knowledge, he told himself. You've got to prove that you know more than she does or at least persuade her that you do. And it has to be something of immediate use.

As yet there had been no mention of a forced gamble as Malvern had claimed but time could be running out. And once in a cage was once too often. Malvern had been lucky to escape and have guides waiting. Even if he left the village Kevin knew that he wouldn't get far. Not even if he managed to steal the lasergun.

Unconsciously he moved closer towards the tent. There would be comfort inside, he thought bitterly. An ultra-sonic device to take care of hungry insects, scented sheets and a pneumatic mattress, cool drinks and decent food. Things which as a fellow Terrestrial she should have been willing to share.

A man rose from the ground and rested the point of his spear against Kevin's chest.

"During the hours of darkness this soil is sacred," he intoned. "Death is the penalty for all who approach the abode of the Seer Into Shadows."

"I am kin," invented Kevin quickly. "I have the right of close association. Her father promised me her hand in marriage."

"Well now," said the guard. "I wouldn't know about that. But my orders are plain."

He pressed forward with the spear. The point sliced through the outer layer of Kevin's laminated blouse and halted as it hit the metal-weave beneath. Grunting he drew back the weapon for another try.

"Hold!" yelled Kevin desperately. "I am protected by the Gods!"

"What the hell's all this noise about?" Crystal stuck her head through the flap of the tent. "Oh, it's you!"

"I've come on an errand of great import," Kevin shouted. "I have had a vision terrifying in its implication. Woe to all if I am not heard! Woe! Woe!"

In one of the tents a child woke, crying. A woman called out, shrill in her anger. A man roared for his spear. The noise began to spread.

"For God's sake!" Crystal jerked open the flap. "Get in here before you wake the village!" Inside she glared at him. "Have you gone crazy? What's this all about?"

She looked radiant in a shimmering negligée of gauzy white, the loose mane of her hair a rippling waterfall of gold as it fell over her shoulders. Her lips were full and soft, the teeth white behind the parted redness. Her eyes frosted with temper.

Impulsively he said; "Crystal, you're beautiful."

"And you're a nurd. You could have got yourself killed out there."

"Would it have bothered you?"

"No," she said. "All right, you're tall and look nice, and if you had brains you'd be quite a man, but so what? The universe is full of men." She cocked her head, listening to the voices outside. "That guard's spreading the news. Did you have to start yakking about visions? These people are superstitious and a thing like that can worry them. Damn you, Blake! Why didn't you get yourself decently killed?"

She meant it, he decided, and felt annoyed. Why did she have to be such a bitch? No girl looking as lovely as she did had a right to be so cold-blooded. Selfish, he told himself. She's too damn selfish. But then the rich always are.

"I came to save your life," he said stiffly. "To warn you of the terrible danger you are in. You may not realise it but you're living on borrowed time."

"You're kooked!"

"I'm serious. Have you studied anthropology? No? Well I have together with a lot of other subjects. In my work you have to have a broad spectrum of wide-based knowledge and I've learned things you probably haven't even heard about. Have you read Velgar's *Rite of the Sun*? Or Keeway's *Magic and Matriarchy*? Or Luminer's *Mystical Motivations of Primitive Tribes*? Even my own recent book touched on the importance of status symbols and the seasonal cycle of influential change. I've studied this village and the nomads and you're walking on thin ice. The writing is on the wall. Your time is running out. The best thing you can do is to pack up and get out while you've got the chance."

"Taking you with me, I suppose?"

"That isn't important," he said earnestly. "I'm thinking of you, Crystal. From the look of things these people are going to move soon. When they do they'll want to be sure of a good spot with plenty of game. How can they be sure of finding it? By sacrifice. By a gift to the Gods. By the best blood of their village spilled on the ground. You're their leader," he said. "Their guide. As such you'll make the best victim. And you're a stranger," he added. "Killing you won't upset anyone and so everyone will be for it. Can you imagine them coming for you? The whole crowd of them all at once. The men will have spears and the women clubs, even the children will carry sticks. They'll chase you around until you drop. I don't know how they'll dispose of you but I can make a guess.

Burn you, perhaps, or tear you apart. Or maybe they'll feed you to some beast, the phren maybe. Whichever way they choose it won't be pleasant. Get out now, Crystal, while you've got the chance!"

Thoughtfully she stared at him, then shook her head. "I've misjudged you, Blake," she said. "I thought you were just a greedy Earthsider who didn't know enough to keep his nose out of other people's business but you're more than that. You're one of the most intelligent and persuasive liars I've ever met. You should become a statesman."

"You don't believe me?"

"No," she said flatly. I don't. I've been propositioned by experts and can tell a con when I see one. It was a good try, Blake, and you've earned yourself a drink, but that's all you're going to get." She poured from a bottle she took from a freezebox and handed him the glass. Lifting her own she said; "Here's health!"

Moodily he drank. A failure, he thought. I'm just a failure. I tried to overwhelm her with the pretence of superior knowledge and she saw right through me. Damn her! But perhaps there was another way?

Holding out his empty glass he said; "That was nice. Could I possibly have another?"

Shrugging, she poured.

"And yourself?" he urged. "Aren't you going to join me?" He smiled as she refilled her own glass. "That's better. I hate to drink alone and it isn't often that I get the chance to share the company of such an attractive and intelligent girl. And you've done so many interesting things that I'd like to hear about. Those cannibals on Beta Syrtis, for instance. And the foot-shrinkers of Khundar. You ought to write a book, sometime. Maybe we could get together on it. I've learned quite a lot about the techniques and could ghost it for you if you like. Where did you go when you first left Earth?"

"You don't give up, do you," she said as he poured more liquor into her glass. "You just keep at it like a dog with a bone."

"I beg your pardon?"

"You're hoping to get me drunk. You want to sit here and get me talking and drinking so that you can take advantage. Right?"

Scowling he said; "Wrong. All I want is my money."

"You're lying again, but never mind. I'm willing to play along. In fact I'll make you a deal. We'll hit the bottle until one of us passes out. If you put me to bed you can have the fruits of victory." Lifting her glass she smiled at him over the rim. "Here's luck."

CHAPTER 8

He didn't put her to bed. Instead Kevin woke with the sun in his eyes, dirt on his face and the taste of dead ants in his mouth. Groggily he climbed to his feet and looked around. The big tent was tightly closed and he vaguely remembered having being thrown out sometime during the second bottle. There were other memories too, the touch of warm lips and rounded flesh, a heady perfume and caressing hands. But that must have been wishful thinking, he decided. An erotic dream induced by the circumstances and sent by the Gods as compensation for unachieved fact.

Blearily he looked around. The village seemed unusually active with little knots of men clustered in deep conversation. Unusually quiet too, even the children seemed to have ceased their eternal racket for which he was grateful. A jar stood outside one of the tents and he picked it up, found it contained water and drank, tipping the remainder over his head. The douche restored him to life. Crystal stocked good booze, he thought. Strong but free of the poisonous ingredients which created such vicious hangovers. That or his stomach had acquired a stronger lining, not surprising considering his recent diet.

The thought of food made him hungry and he crossed to where the women crouched beside the fire. One of them turned and cowered at his approach, lifting one hand in a peculiar gesture. Odd, he thought, up until now they had treated him as if he'd been a somewhat backward child. He tried again and sent them running like a nest of disturbed insects. Thoughtfully he ate a roasted scrap of meat, conscious of the brooding stillness.

Could his invented story have had a basic truth? Was the life of the nomads reaching a climax of some kind? Their actions certainly weren't normal. There should have been shouts and yells, playing, gambling, active contests, boasting, eating, drinking and the eyeing of potential partners. All the activities to which he had become accustomed during his stay. Crystal should know about this.

He turned towards her tent and halted as a native stepped before him. The man held a knife which he promptly dug into Kevin's side.

"What the hell?" He backed as the man poked him in the chest. "You crazy nurd!" Kevin yelled. "What are you doing?"

"Testing," said the man. "Zenmwale claims that you are protected by the Gods. With the full strength of his arm he hurled his spear against you and it penetrated not. Is that so?"

"That is so," admitted Kevin and added, quickly, "But test me not again lest the power that protects me withers your arm. Those beloved of the Gods are not to be treated lightly."

And neither was his blouse, he thought, touching the gashes in the outer layer. The metal-weave had saved him from nasty wounds but he doubted if it would stand up to the slamming impact of a hard-driven spear. The guard had exaggerated, of course. Primitives always did.

"And the vision," said the man as he sheathed his blade. "What is this dreadful portent which sent you crying through the village into the abode of the Seer Into Shadows?"

"Ask her."

"I'm asking you," said the man ominously. "If trouble is coming I want to know about it. I've got a couple of wives and some kids to worry about so I need to know the details. What did you see?"

"I can't tell you," insisted Kevin. "It's a professional confidence."

"You are also a seer?" Absently the native rubbed the insect bites on his brawny throat. "These are strange times," he muttered. "The women grow restless and are slow to obey. The stones bring me no luck and my aim with the spear is not as it was. When my old father, the late chief, was driven crying into the afterlife he swore that he had been deposed by the use of false magic. And now you appear claiming to be a prophet. But the Seer Into Shadows is also a prophet. Of you both who are we to believe?"

"Me," said Kevin hastily. He could guess what might happen to a false claimant to the position. And he was beginning to get an idea. If he could somehow depose Crystal from the top job and take over then she would have no choice but to get them both out of this mess. "I am the true peerer into darkness."

From the crowd which had gathered around a man lunged forward and said; "Can you read the sacred seeds? Can you tell us of what is to come?"

"Sure I can," said Kevin confidently. "What do you want to know?"

"Will my wife bear a son?" called a man.

"Shall I win at the games?"

"Where should I hunt to find plentiful meat?"

"If I marry will my wife be faithful?"

"Am I going to grow old and die in peace?"

"Wait a minute!" yelled Kevin over the babble of voices. "I can't operate standing in the middle of the village like this. I need proper surroundings, equipment, things of great mystery. Gems," he added hopefully. "Rare and precious things of value. Fix me up and I'll see what I can do."

"Hold!" A wizened oldster lifted his arms, halting the rush of the crowd eager to search their belongings. "This is not the way. There are ceremonies to be observed lest we call down the wrath of the Gods and the spite of inimical spirits. This man's mouth is filled with words but who can tell if those words are of meaning? The wind in the trees makes noise but the sounds are empty."

Kevin glared at the opposition. "Are you calling me a liar?"

"You were found a captive," pointed out the old man. "Chained and burdened. Would a man of power have suffered that?"

Without hesitation Kevin said; "It was a time of testing. The Gods needed to be sure that I was worthy and willingly I submitted. Now they have filled me with their promised power. Now the scales have fallen from my eyes and the future is as clear as the waters of a mountain stream.

"Woe unto this village if you spurn the true Seer Into Shadows," he chanted. "Woe! Woe! Woe! Your spears will blunt, the game escape, your wives and children cry hungry for the food you will not be able to find. Weakness shall assail your loins and your women turn and spit on you as less than men. Woe!"

He had shaken them and he could tell it. Even oldster, shrewd as he was, hesitated before speaking. I've beaten him, gloated Kevin. What chance has a nurd like him against a professional dealer in words? Confidently waited for the man to admit his defeat and acknowledge new boss.

Quietly the oldster said; "This man must be tested."

The crowd roared its approval.

"He has come among us and has not yet thrown the sacred stones. The Seer Into Shadows has no doubt her own reasons for the delay but we can delay no longer. There cannot be two prophets in the village. One must go."

"Steady on," said Kevin, shaken. "What are you talking about? What's all this business about a test?" Uneasily he remembered Malvern and his story of the dice. What would happen if he lost? And suppose he won, what would happen to the girl? "Can't we just forget all about it?" he asked. "I mean, what's the point? Aren't two prophets better one?"

"Who could we trust?" said the oldster reasonably. "If one is genuine then why bother to support two? Anyway we have to be sure of your powers. First you prophesy and then, if you prove out, you and the Seer Into Shadow will cast the sacred stones. The winner will become our leader."

"And the loser?"

"Well now," grinned the oldster. "If you're as good as you claim you won't have to worry about that."

* * * *

Crystal picked up a bottle and threw it savagely to the ground. Glass splintered, shards flying through the air one of them doing more damage to his blouse. "You idiot!" she stormed. "You stupid nurd! I told you these people were superstitious! Is it impossible for you to control the flapping of that big mouth?"

Offended he said; "I had no choice."

"Like hell you didn't! Of all the things to think of you had to claim to be a prophet! Couldn't you have told them you'd had a dream and left it at that? Couldn't you have given the impression that you were crazy?" Snatching up a second bottle she flung it after the first. "Do you realise just what you've got yourself into?"

She's worried, he thought, leaning back and looking around the interior of the big tent. I've managed to shake her position and she doesn't want to lose her job. Well, what did she expect? I'm not an ignorant savage willing to believe in her lies. I'm not impressed by a few scientific gimmicks. I'll win the test, he decided, and then I'll let her sweat for a while. Just like she did me.

She glared at him, tall and lovely in her ceremonial robe, a glittering headdress rising above the gold of her hair. "Well?"

"All this is your own fault," he said reasonably. "If you'd given me my money and provided a couple of guides I'd have been gone by now. As it is I've got to do things my way. But I won't be as nasty as you were," he added generously. "When I'm the head man I'll take care of you. You can even share this tent if you like."

"That's damned decent of you," she sneered.

"I'm a decent type of man."

"You're a fool! I'll bet Ansher put you up to this. That old guy's been after my job since I won it. He doesn't like women anyway and he's got a lot of support." She frowned, thinking. "I've got a drug," she suggested. "I could give it to you and you'd appear to be dead. They'd dump you beyond the village and, when you came to, you could get away."

Firmly he shook his head. "No."

"It's the best way out," she urged. "I'll give you some supplies and you can have the lasergun. With luck you could make it."

"No," he said again. "I haven't got that kind of luck. Anyway, what are you scared of? I'll make some prophecies and that's all there is to it. By the time they've found out if they're any good or not we can be well away. We can tell them we have to go into the forest to communicate with the spirits, or something. Threaten to put a curse on anyone who follows." He relaxed, grinning. "Simple. I wish I'd thought of it before."

"Look outside," she said curtly. "Go on, look!"

The tent was surrounded by a ring of men carrying spears. They had the air of men conducting serious business.

"They're not going to let us go anywhere," Crystal said as Kevin returned to his seat. "You've got to go through with it, first the prophecy and then the test. I'm sorry, Blake, but it's all your own fault. Is there any you'd like me to deliver for you after you're gone?"

"Gone?"

"Dead. Shall I let your wife know? Your girlfriend? It's no trouble," she urged. "I won't be sticking around for much longer anyway. I'm getting a little bored."

"I haven't got a wife," he said bleakly. Nor a girlfriend, he told himself, no matter what Julia thought. In fact there was no one who would give a damn if he simply vanished. Ransom, maybe, but to the agent he was only a name in a ledger. A stroke of the pen and he would be written out. Tarvainen? Duncan? Felicita Marmot? To them he was just someone they had once met. Of all the teeming billions of Earth there wasn't a single person who would miss him.

A writer's life is a lonely one, he thought sombrely. But did Crystal have to be so damned casual about his demise?

"We've got to face facts," she said when he protested. "You haven't a chance of winning the test. And you won't be given time for any prophecy you make to be really checked out. They just want to see you perform. You've got to impress them with your supposed powers. If they like it, all right, but you will have to be tested to determine if you are genuine or not. Primitives are practical people," she explained. "If you're favoured of the Gods you'll win. If not then you'll lose and they'll get rid of you fast because you'll be bad luck and a bad influence."

"This test," he said thoughtfully. "The old guy said something about casting the sacred stones. Who does the throwing?"

"I do."

"Dice?"

"That's right. We do it after you've performed which won't be until this evening. In the meantime you'd better relax. Would you like drink?"

"No thanks," he said quickly, remembering her previous suggestion. Who knew what she might slip into the booze? "I've got some thinking to do."

It was a long day. As the sun began to lower behind the trees the ceremony began. In solemn procession they marched through the village, first Crystal, resplendent in her costume, carrying a carved wooden box and by men with spears. Then Kevin, some elders, the oldster, Ansher, grinning all over his face and wearing what seemed to be a coating of blood and dung, a dozen drummers, three men with flutes, all accompanied by the ubiquitous spear bearers.

Three times they circled the tents and shacks then finally halted before the abode of the Seer Into Shadows. The drummers spread themselves into a circle, their fingers caressing the taut skins, creating a low susurration, mysterious, inimical. The flutes yielded a muted wail. Behind the drummers, controlled by the spearmen, the men and women of the village thronged close. A man produced a chair on which Crystal sat. Light from the fires reflected from her glittering head-dress, touched her hair with scarlet and amber.

Handing the carved box to Kevin she said: "All right, genius. Let's see what you can do."

Taking the box he squatted cross-legged on the ground and opened it. Inside rested a couple of dozen ovoids each about an inch long, dark and worn with time and manipulation. They bore faded symbols; lines, circles, crosses, triangles, a cross-hatched mishmash as if a child had scratched at them with a sharp point. Confidently he closed the box, shook it, opened the lid and spilled the seeds to the ground.

Broodingly he studied them.

They made no sense at all, lying in a jumble on the dirt, the faint marks almost invisible in the gathering gloom. He leaned closer, giving the appearance of wrapt attention, wondering just what the hell was expected. Should he stiffen, go into a fake trance? Or would it be better to appear nonchalant as if this was a tired old familiar business? Cautiously he reached out to touch the seeds, halting the motion of his arm at the sound of indrawn breath. Wrong? He let his finger run from one of the ovoids to the other, remembering Felicita's party, the guff he had got away with when giving the valuation of her artistic creation.

If he could fool sophisticates these natives would be a piece of cake.

"I see a great darkness," he intoned after letting the tension mount. "A time of gloom and shadows when the sun will hide its face from the eyes of men and terror will stalk the forest. The hills will wear blackness and become as one with chaos. Death will lurk in the trees and spring ravening from the ground. Woe to those who walk abroad in that dreadful time! Woe! Woe! But the darkness will pass and light again return to the hills. The sky will glow with the bright radiance of the sun and the shadows vanish as if they had never been. The beasts and terrors which lurk in the forest will be stilled and the air will shine with brilliance. Then may the men walk abroad protected from the things of dreadful darkness by the power of light. All this do I read in the sacred seeds."

The drums roared to a crescendo. Under the cover of the noise Crystal said, sarcastically; "So you've told them night is coming and that day will follow. Some prophet!"

Sweating Kevin glared at the ovoids. If the damned runes meant anything he hadn't a clue as to what it was. Improvise, he told himself. Elaborate. Say anything as long as it's impressive. If he didn't Crystal would shoot him down.

"Hold!" he yelled as the drums faded back into their rolling susurration. "I see death!" He lifted his head and he stared at the circle of faces. He pointed to one at random. "If you should go into the forest to hunt as is in your mind, beware! Your spear will break and your bones whiten on the dirt. For five days must you stay within your tent and offer sacrifices to the Gods. Who among you have bearing children?" A cluster of hands shot into the air. "You will have a son," he said at random, pointing also. "You will have twin girls and you a daughter. You and you will have sons." He rattled off the specific information, safe enough as he wouldn't be around long enough for the proof to arrive.

As the drums thundered again Ansher pushed himself forward. "You spoke of a great danger to the village," he reminded. "Have the sacred seeds told you of what is to come?"

The nurd! thought Kevin. He's trying to pin me down. This has got to be good.

Muttering he stared at the seeds then reared, arm voice rising above the drums.

"There will come a time of change," he said loudly. "The spirits have cursed this place and doom is moving closer with the passing of each day. Soon it will arrive and death and desolation will walk among you. Your tents will be empty and the wail of the women will echo over your bones. The winds will sigh over emptiness and the beasts will feed on the flesh of your children. All this will happen unless you obey the will of the gods. Go! Rise and move! In five days," he added hastily, remembering his previous prophecy. "Five days in which you must prepare. Five days in which no man shall spill the blood of another. Five days of preparation and then, as the sun touches the tips of the highest trees, you will move fifty miles to the west. There you will find a place in which seven trees form a circle and there you will stay." He lowered his voice and said, sombrely: "The Sacred Seeds have spoken. All the rest lies in darkness."

"Not bad," said Crystal as the drums sent echoes over the village. "Not bad at all. And now, genius, are you ready for the test?" Lifting her voice she called. "Bring forth the sacred bones!"

There was no way to dodge it. Ansher pressed close carrying a small box which rattled as he set it down. Crystal dipped into it and held up a pair of dice. Modern, dice, noted Kevin, plastic cubes of ruby redness the spots shining flecks of gold. Inwardly he steeled himself.

"Here." She threw them towards him. "Toss for first go. You know the rules? You get a seven before I do. Go ahead."

He rolled the bones, a five. "You win," she said as she cast a three. "Go ahead."

He reached for the dice with his left hand, kept his right moving and grabbed her by the wrist, cupping her own palm in his own. He grinned as he felt the expected cubes. Sliding back his hand he dragged them from her palm, cupping them in his own, bringing his left hand up with the other set. Holding them firm between the fleshy part of his thumb and palm he rattled the others and tossed them down.

A seven. He wasn't surprised.

* * * *

"Loaded dice," he said. "How low can you get?"

"Quit crowing," she snapped. "You won. What more you want?"

He sat down, smiling, looking around the tent with a proprietary air. Outside the night was torn by the roar of drums, the shadows of capering men leaping over the fabric. It was a time of celebration. The old prophet was deposed and with her the bad influence which had affected the women of the tribe. Now they would have to obey. The new Seer Into Shadows was a man and would soon put an end to all that nonsense about equality. Now, for five days, they had nothing to do but enjoy themselves, safe from the impending doom, secure in the possession of a tried and tested seer.

Kevin felt good. Without asking he helped himself to a drink and relaxed. In five days anything could happen but one thing he was sure of. He wouldn't be around long enough to see it.

Sipping he said; "Loaded dice. So much for the truth of the Gods."

"You knew," she accused.

"I guessed. You're too smart to have trusted luck. Anyway, I wrote a book about gamblers once, how they cheat and how they manipulate. Would you like a drink?"

"That's damned decent of you," she said bitterly. "Considering it's mine."

"For five days," he reminded, enjoying his victory. "Then you get the chop. Is there anything you'd like me to do for you? A message you'd like me to send to your husband or boyfriend? A last word to your dear old father, perhaps? It's no trouble."

"Go to hell!" Fuming she changed, stripping off the ceremonial garments, dressing in pants, blouse and boots similar to his own, apparently oblivious of his appreciative stare. "You're not going to have me killed."

Which was true enough though he had no intention of saying so. Let her writhe for a while and then, when she asked nicely, he would put her mind at rest. Pointedly he said: "What about Malvern?"

"Who?" She shrugged when he told her. "Oh, him? A drunk who couldn't keep his hands to himself. I had to go through the motions but I gave him his chance. He escaped, didn't he?"

"And the old chief?"

"That was different. He knew what it was all about and took his chances. Anyway, he had the idea that I should become his sixth wife." Impatiently she strode about the tent. "Never mind him. What do you intend to do about me?"

Deliberately he took another drink. Not nice enough, he decided. Let her wait for a day, certainly until morning, then he might be gracious. In fact, he mused, looking at her, the situation might hold an unexpected bonus. A terrified, pleading girl might think it best to appeal to his emotions. Not that she looked terrified but give her time. It must be hard for a girl like her to have to admit defeat.

"Nice brandy," he said lifting the glass. "You have good taste."

"I've a lot more than that," she said meaningfully, stepping close. "You'd be a fool to let them kill me."

"I would?"

"Daddy won't pay unless you deliver. How much did he promise you, by the way?" She shook her head when he told her. "Always the cheapskate. Hold out for double, you'll get it."

"We made a deal," he said stiffly. "I couldn't do that. Anyway, he wouldn't come across."

"Yes he would." She looked up as a roar came from outside and frenzied yells split the night. Going to the flap she looked outside. "Ansher's working them up to something," she said, returning. "Can you use a lasergun?"

Startled, he put down the glass. "Will I have to?"

More yells came before she could answer. The flap jerked open and the oldster pranced inside. Sweat had made the dung and blood run in weird patterns, his eyes were glazed and his breath held the odour of primitive beer.

"I denounce you!" he yelled. "False prophet I denounce you! One of the men you told would have a son has a girl-child instead. Is it thus that you read the Sacred Seeds?"

Dammit! thought Kevin sickly. One of those women jumped the gun. Why the hell didn't I think that maybe one of them was about due?

"They must die!" shouted Ansher. "Both must die to appease the affronted Gods. Thus it is that they tell us neither is a true prophet. The woman will burn and the man feed the phren!"

"Now wait a minute," said Kevin. "Let's not be hasty about this. Would you like a drink?"

"At dawn!" gloated the old man. "When the sun rises we shall make sacrifice. Guards, hold them close!"

They surged forward then halted as a smoking line appeared at their feet. Lasergun in hand Crystal stood at the rear of the tent. Again she fired and men gaped at their headless spears.

"Witness the power of the Gods," yelled Kevin taking advantage of the moment. "Go before you are stricken as your spears. Go!"

Ansher dragged his feet. "It is a weapon," he accused. "Soon its power will be exhausted. And the finger of death can only point in one direction at a time. See if it will protect you when the sun dazzles your eyes." He spat and then hastily withdrew as Crystal lifted the lasergun.

"Shrewd," said Kevin, shakily as he helped himself to brandy. "That old coot isn't as simple as he makes out. You should have cut him down."

"And then what?" Crystal stood the lasergun against the table and helped herself to a drink. "We can't escape in the dark and I'm low on charges. Start killing and they'll be on us like a swarm of bees. Well, genius? What do you suggest?"

Baffled he went to the flap and squinted through the opening, seeing firelight glint on edged metal. They were ringed by a forest of spears. Beyond the guards shapes leaped in mounting frenzy excited at the prospect of the fun to come. Fun for them, of course. His skin crawled as he thought about it. "Damn it," he said. "This morning they seemed so civilised. So reasonable. Surely they won't kill us?"

Crystal shrugged, amazingly cool. "You heard the man. This has given him the opportunity he's been waiting for. Me deposed and you proved a phoney. All he has to do now is to walk in and take over. Damn it, Blake, why did you have to be so smart? Had you lost the throw I could have done something about it. Now start thinking."

"We'll move," he decided. "Pack up a few things and we'll get going just before dawn. I'll take the lasergun and cover the retreat. You head into the forest and lie low until it's day. I'll join you if I can."

"My hero," she said. "And then?"

"We'll keep moving downhill. We'll have to come out somewhere." He glared at her amused expression. "Have you a better idea?"

"You bet," she said calmly. "I've a radio and a pilot on standby. I'll just tell him to come and pick us up."

CHAPTER 9

Finch came into his office, rubbing his hands, beaming. "Well, well," he said. "It's a real pleasure to see you again, Miss Tarvainen. A real pleasure. Have a nice trip?"

"Lousy," said Kevin.

The factor ignored him. "Your pilot tells me that there was a little rumpus when he picked you up. Nothing serious, I hope?"

"Just a little local fun," said Crystal. "Nothing to worry about."

"You didn't have to kill anyone? No? Good!" Finch looked relieved. "Not that it would matter all that much but it's best to avoid complications. The natives are funny, a bunch of savages but they want to keep them intact. For the tourist trade," he explained. "It's an attraction. Visit the real, primitive life of the Blue Hills. Illagesh is getting ambitious." He looked at Kevin. "Where's Malvern?"

"Dead. Your sweet natives," said Kevin. "The guides. They took off his head and then took off with all we owned."

"Too bad." Finch shook his head. "I liked Malvern. A real drinking man. Well, I'll pass the word but I don't suppose it will do any good. They've probably gone over to Lake Dengue. A real nest of cut-throats over there. So you had a nice time, Miss Tarvainen?"

"It wasn't too bad," she said casually, looking at Kevin. "Especially towards the end. Right, hero?"

He scowled, remembering his mounting anxiety as they'd waited for rescue, his relief when it finally came. He'd felt a fool standing there, lasergun in hand, steeling himself to die beneath a shower of spears. And he felt a bigger fool for not realising that she would have an easy way out all the time. It was glaringly logical when you thought about it. No woman with her money would have ignored the obvious. But she could have told him. A sadist, he decided. Just like he'd heard from Malvern. A warped, twisted nature which delighted in seeing a man squirm.

"Well, Miss Tarvainen," said Finch, "what are your plans? A group of Kalitieds have bought a thousand square miles on the lower continent and are setting up a biofactory for the manufacture of big game. There'll be some good hunting soon. Or there's the rain festival almost due at Geshel in the second quadrant."

"I think I'll be moving on," she said. "You'll let me know when anything decent arrives in the way of transportation?"

"Sure, Miss Tarvainen. You'll be staying at the Splendide? I'll take care of your things. You want me to call a rickshaw?"

"Wait a minute," snapped Kevin. "What about my money?"

"Money?" She looked at him, smiling. "Did I take any money from you?"

"No, but—"

"And I supplied transportation back here from the village. Don't you think that's worth something?" Her eyes grew hard, calculating. "Sorry, Blake, but I play hard rules. Of course, if you were to ask very nicely I might spare you a little for bed and board. Enough for a couple of days, say, to give you time to look around. Well?"

"Damn you," he said harshly. "Keep your lousy charity. I'll make my own way."

It was easier said than done. Bleakly he watched as the factor escorted the girl to a rickshaw then headed for the landing field. It was almost deserted. A stained craft sat with sealed ports on the dirt. A private pleasure ship had three stern toadstools on guard who warned him to stay well away; the owner was sporofulating. A scaled creature in a water-filled suit worked with a welding torch on the plates of a leaking tramp. The only feasible vessel was from the worlds of Salasuund carrying a complement of owls from Twhoot.

"Passage?" The purser ruffled its feathers and blinked thoughtful eyes. "Well, now, we're a chartered vessel on an educative trip but I guess it could be arranged if you didn't mind sleeping in a nest and eating the normal diet of worms, snakes and small mammals. How much can you afford?"

"Nothing," said Kevin. "I'd hoped to be allowed to work my passage," he explained. "I'm a pretty good hand when it comes to clearing up. And I can entertain. Stories of ancient Earth, tales of adventure, sagas and epic poems."

"Forget it," snapped the purser.

"How about grooming, then? I'm a good feather-man."

Angrily the bird snapped its beak. "You're a scrounger," it said. "A bum. A dirty egg-eater. Get going before I claw you."

Finch met him as he left the field. "You can flop in my office if you're stuck," he volunteered. "And you can eat too if you're willing to do a little work. I don't like to see a fellow man on his beam ends."

"Thanks," said Kevin gratefully. "I'll think about it."

"Got something in mind?"

"I'll look around for a while. Maybe I can get fixed up in town."

It was a slim hope as he soon found. Jobs were mostly given to the locals who were accustomed to low pay and the best he could find was a clerking job at starvation wages. He left promising to think it over. Back in the street he found it had started to rain and ran for cover into a hotel. It was the Splendide, the one Crystal was staying at, the one he had himself used when first he'd arrived and still had money.

Heading for the lounge he sat and waved aside the girl who came to serve him. "Later," he promised. "I'm expecting company."

"But, sir! It is not permitted—"

"Later!" he snapped.

She bowed and moved away with a faint chiming of bells. A charming girl, he thought. Attentive, on the job, eager to serve. He hoped that she didn't guess his true condition. The hotel didn't cater to penniless transients who came in to escape the rain.

Money, he brooded. How different life was if you had it. Crystal, now, she didn't know what it was to go without. She was probably enjoying a cool drink in the bar at this very moment, or eating, or soaking in a nice, hot bath, or resting in one of the comfortable beds while he sat here waiting to be thrown out.

Shabalan? Kevin wondered if it would be worth approaching the advocate. The native hadn't given the impression of being generous but maybe, as one professional man to another? Regretfully Kevin dismissed the idea. As a supposed top-flight Terrestrial lawyer what would he be doing without funds?

Damn it! What was he going to do?

He tensed as a tall native came towards him. The man was polite but firm.

"Sir, are you a resident of this hotel?"

"I was," said Kevin. "I might be later."

"But not now? I see. Do you require refreshment then? Or could I summon the person for whom you are waiting?"

"Miss Crystal Tarvainen," said Kevin desperately. "You know her?"

"No, sir. I have seen her, that is all. Is she the person for whom you wait?"

"That's right," said Kevin and added, boldly. 'You had better bring me a pot of tisane."

Before it arrived he was at the desk asking for Crystal's room number, brain aflame with a brilliant idea. He had forgotten the literal mindedness of the Illageshian culture and, after her sojourn among the savages Crystal might have forgotten it too. Now, if only she wasn't in the bar or dining room— She wasn't and he climbed the stairs to her room, collecting a couple of chambermaids on the way. Outside her door he paused, listening, hearing the splash of running water.

"Sir!" One of the maids protested as he lifted his foot. "Sir, you should knock and wait an answer."

Ignoring the protest he slammed his foot against the panel, lunging forward as it burst open. Crystal stared at him from where she stood naked before the shower.

"Dear God, you again!" she stormed. "What the hell do you want?"

* * * *

The shuttle was a brand new vessel of the Keelab—Shwain—Elgar—Fhrome circuit and the skipper was proud to have such a distinguished passenger. "My dear, Miss Tarvainen," he beamed. "Welcome to the *Argentis*. If there is any little thing I can do for you please don't hesitate to ask. And your friend, too," he added, his eyes flicking to where Kevin sat beside the girl. "We shall be leaving within the hour."

"Direct to Fhrome," reminded Kevin happily. "A pity you can't go direct to Earth."

"It could be arranged," said the skipper meaningfully. "The expense would be high, naturally, but it could be arranged."

"Never mind," snapped Crystal. "We can tranship at Fhrome. In the meanwhile I'd like a couple of bottles of brandy. My companion has something to celebrate," she explained waspishly. "Or he thinks he has."

"Your promise to accompany me to Earth," agreed Kevin as the skipper hurried to accommodate his passenger. "You to pay all expenses. My travelling money back. Yes, I guess I do have cause to celebrate. But not with brandy. I've no intention of getting drunk."

"But I have," she fumed. "To be caught by a trick like that! I should have fought it. Gone to court. You'd never have made it stick."

Perhaps not, thought Kevin with satisfaction, but it had been a chance she hadn't been willing to take. The oral promise had been plain and he'd had a couple of witnesses No matter what the circumstances had been he'd had a good case and she knew it. She hadn't even appealed to a local advocate for an opinion. Instead, after a long argument, she'd given in. The shuttle had arrived that very evening and now they were on their way.

Earth, he thought. Good, old Mother Earth. There was no place like it especially if you had money. I'll have a vacation at Polar North, he promised himself. Buy a lease on a decent apartment where I won't have to share. Get a new typewriter and really settle down to write. A genuine book, he decided. One filled with real characters, and am brimming with poignant emotion, sparkling with stomach-gripping action and hinting at tremendous moral implications. An allegorical message for the people of his time with scintillating dialogue and inspiring narrative. It would be the best-seller of the century with people quoting from it and producers begging to be given the chance to buy screen rights. It would be reprinted all over the entire galaxy and beings of all races would fight for the chance to meet the author.

He woke with a start and looked at the brimming glass Crystal held towards him.

"Come on," she urged. "Let's be friendly. I'll admit you got the better of me but there's no hard feelings. Join me in a drink."

Tempted he almost fell then firmly shook his head.

"Kevin," she breathed, using the name for the first time "Have I ever told you how handsome you are? How tall and strong and admirable? When you stood in that village ready to die to protect me you looked superb. I shall never forget it."

"Neither shall I," he said, thinking of the aftermath. "Now shut up and let me sleep."

"How can I do that?" she demanded. "I'm bored and need to talk. Damn it, you don't have to be so nasty, do you? Where's the harm in a little drink? Come on, hero, I hate to drink alone."

Sighing he accepted the glass and took a cautious sip. It tasted as it should but how could he be certain it hadn't been spiked? He couldn't, he decided, and, as if by accident, spilled it on the floor.

"Clumsy," she chided, smiling. "Take mine."

Ignoring the offer he reached for the unopened bottle noting that its companion was almost empty. Startled he glanced at his watch surprised to discover how long he had slept.

"You don't trust me," Crystal said as he opened the sealed bottle and poured himself a small drink. "You think I'm going to do you down in some way."

"Well, aren't you?" he demanded. "We're not on Illagesh now and so their law doesn't apply. You'll walk out on me at the first opportunity you get."

"Not you," she purred. "I'd never walk out on you, Kevin. Not now. I've been watching you while you were asleep. Did you know that you've a wonderful profile? How is it that a handsome man like you has no wife?"

She was drunk, he decided. That or pretending to be. How else account for her sudden change? The maudlin expression in her eyes? She's conning me, he thought bleakly. Trying to persuade me that I mean something to her, letting me know that she's in love with me. He felt a bitter regret that it couldn't possibly be true, that it was all part of an elaborate scheme to break her given word. Irritably he swallowed the brandy.

"That's better," she said softly refilling his glass. "Now you're relaxing as you should. Just as if you'd been working all day and the stint was over and you'd sat down and I was pouring you a drink and telling you that dinner wouldn't be long and where should we go afterwards? To a theatre, maybe, or to call on friends or have them call on us. And we could talk about your latest novel and how the children were getting on and—"

"Shut up!"

"Why, Kevin, darling!" Her eyes were mirrors of innocence. "Don't you like me to talk to you that way?"

Too damn much, he thought and said; "Let's talk of other things if you've got to keep yakking. What was that six-set like?"

"The group I joined in marriage?" She shrugged. "Not what you think. It was a meeting of minds in an inter-racial commune and my job was to act as mediator in domestic arguments. Local law was funny about living together and so we all got married. A crazy set-up, really, but it was fun for the week it lasted. Another drink, darling?"

"No. What made you leave Earth in the first place?"

"Can't you remember what it's like? All those people, no clean air, living like ants all the time. I got bored," she said thoughtfully. "Nothing but parties and stupid conversation and a bunch of phonies hanging around. I tried to do some social work but that was just as bad. You start by giving favours and end by meeting demands. So I took a short trip to another world. Then I moved on and just kept moving. Maybe I'm looking for something," she said ambiguously. "A psychologist told me that once. He could have been right."

"Looking for what?"

She leaned closer towards him, body soft as it contacted his own, perfume wafting into his nostrils. "Who knows?" she asked softly. "Adventure, perhaps? Romance. A place in which to be happy." Her hand lifted and rubbed against his blouse. "A man to be happy with."

For how long, he thought sourly. Until the novelty died? Then she'd be up and away with her money leaving the poor nurd to make the best of it. By a tremendous effort of will he remained detached, fighting the impulse to take her into his arms, to kiss the soft lips, to snap at the proffered bait. She's a bitch, he reminded himself. A scheming, crafty character you'd be a fool to trust. Remember the village, the way she stole your money, the indifference in which she left you stranded? One wrong step now and you'll be right back where you started. Hang on and collect from Tarvainen.

Money, he thought, closing his eyes. Beautiful money. What was a woman against that?

* * * *

At Fhrome, wide awake and tinglingly alert, he went shopping for transportation to Earth. Crystal dragged at his side, fighting the hand he kept firmly clamped around her wrist, eyes snapping with anger. "You don't have to do that," she stormed. "I've given you my word. You don't have to treat me as if I were a prisoner."

"You're not a prisoner," he said. "I regard you as a precious possession and I'd hate to lose you in the crowd. Now why don't you be sensible and walk quietly side?"

To his surprise she obeyed, walking demurely beside him as he thrust his way through the assembled touts, agents, travellers and assorted life-forms which were the inevitable conglomeration of every spacefield. Fhrome was a busy junction with vessels of a dozen types thickly scattered over the ground, the air humming with a variety of sounds. It was also very hot and Kevin paused to ease his collar and mop his face with his free hand.

"Blake, you're a fool," said Crystal. "Why don't you trust me? We could stay at a hotel for a few days, rest up, get some clothes and have a vacation. The Starman Rest is a good hotel. They have a swimming pool, environmental conditioning in every room and the finest drinks in this part of the galaxy. I'll book us a suite and we could take it easy."

Firmly Kevin shook his head. "No."

"Why not?" she urged. "What's the hurry? A few days can't make any difference."

"You're trying to bribe me," he said. "It isn't going to work. We're going to Earth whether you like it or not shut up while I look for a ship."

"Damn you, Blake," she said. And screamed.

It was a shrill, ear-twisting sound, which scraped at the nerves and set his teeth on edge. The attention-ca Shlemian wail-singer. On all sides beings turned and stared, hair, fur, antennae, and eye-stalks bristling. A burly trog stepped forward sucking at his tusks.

"You having trouble, lady? This character offending you?"

"Get lost!" snapped Kevin. "This woman is my wife. You want to come between us?"

"Not me," said the trog quickly. "That's a thing I never do. She been acting up?"

"Ran off with a lousy Phiparian dancer," said Kevin. "Left me and three kids to manage as best we might. I've only just caught up with her." He jerked his head towards the assembled vessels. "Know a ship due to leave for Earth?"

"Let me go!" shouted Crystal. "Let me go you savage!" She sucked in her breath preparatory to another scream.

"Smack her on the skull," advised the trog as Kevin clamped his hand over her mouth. "There's no point in being gentle with a woman. One good crack and they fall into line. That's the way to treat a wife. I've had three," he added. "Take it from me, it works every time."

"You heard the man?" Kevin snatched his hand away from biting teeth. "Now behave or I'll do just what he says." To his new-found friend he said, "What about that ship?"

The trog jerked his thumb towards a glowing ellipsoid at the side of the field. "You could try the *Planana*. Arachnids but they aren't too bad if you don't mind riding in a web. Or there's the *Skreltash*. That's the one shaped like a double-cone. Cats but decent enough if you aren't allergic to fur. Or there's the *Ullalla*. Pricey but fast and with a humanoid crew. The steward's a friend of mine. Tell him Oogh sent you and he'll look after you." He glanced at Crystal. "A smack on the skull," he reminded. "Don't you forget it."

"I won't," promised Kevin and went looking for the recommended vessel. It was a trim craft crewed by blue-skinned Wendarians, man-sized creatures with stunted horns and prehensile noses. The steward was accommodating.

"Sure I can fix you up," he said. "Any friend of Oogh's a friend of mine. You'll want a cabin, of course?"

"Yes," said Crystal.

Kevin beamed.

"I've got just the thing," said the steward happily as he ushered them into the ship. "A nice double. Soft mattress, hypnotic screen with choice of programme, adjustable environmental control, mist-shower and a vending machine built right into the wall." He opened the door with a flourish. "There!"

It was a beautiful cabin. Kevin stared at the wide, soft bed, the shower, the joys offered in the vending machine. The trip to Earth, he decided, would be a pleasure. A few drinks from the machine, a nice meal, a shower whenever he felt like it, and the chance to get a really get a decent rest. And Crystal, of course, he couldn't forget the girl. After all she was paying for it. And he wouldn't be offensive. If she insisted he would let her have the cabin for her sole use whenever she wanted it.

"I'll take it," said Crystal and spoilt it all by adding, "Alone."

"Madam?" The tip of the steward's nose lifted inquiringly.

"You heard me," said Crystal. "I'll take it for my own use."

Bitterly Kevin demanded, "What about me?"

"You can ride in the lounge."

"Now wait a minute," he snapped. "This is stupid. You're paying for a double so why can't we use it? At least we can take turns using the bed and shower. And if you don't like that why can't we have a pair of singles?"

"There are no vacant singles," said the steward. "I'm sorry but that's the only cabin we have."

"And I'm taking it," said Crystal. "I'm paying," she reminded Kevin. "I promised you transport but you'll take what I give you. The cabin for me and you can travel with the rest. Now get out of here while I take a shower."

Breathing hard Kevin obeyed. The steward, nose still uplifted, led the way to the lounge and there left Kevin to make his own way. A spined cactus wearing belts of silver mesh pointedly made room in the crowded compartment and he squeezed cautiously into the vacant seat. Facing him a slug toyed with an elaborate assembly of rods, wires and swinging objects while next to the creature an octopod wove a something from a tangle of coloured threads.

"For the Harmonic Circle," it explained, catching Kevin's eye. "You have heard of Quallzen customs? We sit in a circle, eight of us, one for each of the Mystic Limbs, and we concentrate on the Great Harmony. This fabrication will serve as a guide to our thoughts, leading them along the One True Path to a finer appreciation of the Harmonic Whole. You have a similar rite, perhaps?"

"No," said Kevin shortly.

"Then perhaps you would wish me to elaborate?"

Kevin restrained a visible shudder, a tedious conversation on the aspects of other-world religions was something he could do without. In defence he looked at the thing the slug held in its extruded pseudopods.

"This is a most interesting device," said the slug. It wore a robe of vivid scarlet with a pouched belt and cap of tasselled silk in emerald green. "The object is to so arrange the suspended items that they will strike a pleasing chord when shaken. They must also add to a prime numb no matter in which direction they are counted. The secret is, naturally, that when one has the correct juxtaposition the chord will automatically follow. Or, if you are more musical than mathematical the correct solution can be found by a discerning ear. I hope to interest certain manufacturers in its production."

"Is that so," said Kevin.

"Yes," said the slug. "An ingenious fabrication, is it not? An instrument which could relieve the tedium of space travel and all delays in the conducting of business together with any periods of waiting attending, perhaps, the birth-cycle of various races. One from which great profits could be made. Merely by chance, of course, I happen to have a portion of the discovery available to anyone who would care to invest. You would be interested in a licence to manufacture, perhaps?"

"No thank you."

"Or maybe you would care to act as agent on your own world? For a quick contract the fee would be most reasonable."

"I am sure it would," said Kevin. "And it pains me that I am unable to take advantage of your offer." Beside him the cactus rustled its spines.

"I too have a most amusing device," it rasped. An educational toy based on sequential colours. Perhaps we could arrange a mutual exchange?"

Kevin closed his eyes and did his best to close his ears against the gush of production costs, potential markets, profit margins, specialised selling against blanket promotions, percentages and intrinsic value of materials.

CHAPTER 10

Half-way to Earth Kevin yawned, stretched and jerked awake uneasily conscious that something was wrong. The lounge was almost empty, only a family of Bubaccks sitting hunched over an incense pot and a few assorted creatures lying comatose in their chairs. Rising he moved towards the girl's cabin and found it deserted. The exit port was open, warm, scented air wafting in from the world outside. Frantically he searched for the steward.

"The girl? Where is she?"

"Why, outside, sir. It is the custom when we land for passengers to stretch their appendages and this is a most interesting world. We shall be here for another—"

"Why didn't you waken me?" demanded Kevin.

"Your mate gave instructions that you were not to be disturbed, sir. I understood that a somnolent condition was essential to your life-cycle and—"

Kevin didn't wait to hear the rest. He dived for the exit ignoring the shouts from behind. To hell with the prophylactic injections. He'd take his chance on contracting ergot, rust, scale-rot or whatever. Outside he glared around.

Nothing. Plenty of creatures of all shapes and sizes, mounds of what appeared to be fungi rearing from beyond the limits of the spaceport, a host of peddlers offering trinkets for sale but not a sign of Crystal Tarvainen.

"You want nice object as memento, sir?" squeaked a native. It looked like a mobile cauliflower. "Very decorative. Good conversation piece. Very inexpensive."

"Have you seen an Earthgirl?" snapped Kevin. "Like me," he explained. "But wearing different clothes and with long, blonde hair."

"You like piece of petrified moss shaped in most pleasing pattern? Or maybe a rare and valuable jar of warring spores?"

"The girl! Have you seen her?"

"I have delicate fabrication of subtle beauty for reluctant sale," squeaked the native with dogged persistence. "You may become proud owner of same for ridiculous price of—"

Kevin darted away not waiting to learn the details of the incredible bargain. From the crowd he guessed that the ship hadn't been here long which gave him a thin chance of finding the girl before she got wholly away. Beyond the field straggled a collection of low huts and plaster houses. He went through them like a wind, ignoring the hums, chirps, squeaks and grunts of irritation which followed his thrusting progress. More time was lost in questioning the taciturn owners of local vehicles. Still more in discovering that the usual crowd of touts knew even less than he did. Finally he paused, gasping, mopping his streaming face and neck.

Think, he told himself firmly. Stop and think instead of rushing around like a crazy fool. Where would she have gone? Who would have seen her? Helped her, even. What would he do if he were on the run, had money and just wanted to stay out of sight for a while? Bribed someone to let him stay in a room? She could be there now, he thought bitterly. Watching him, maybe, laughing at him for having been such an idiot. Damn the girl! Didn't she know that he couldn't leave without her?

"You in trouble, son?" Kevin turned. A man stood watching him from beneath the brim of a faded hat. He was old, dressed in thin fabrics, his face seamed and wrinkled like a prune. "You look kind of flustered," he said. "And you created quite a stir. The natives think you might have gone crazy."

Kevin scowled. "What's it to you?"

"I'm the Terran agent here, son. They figure I'm sort of responsible for others of my own race. You come in on the *Ullalla*?"

"That's right."

"A fine ship, son. Good, fast and clean. Maybe you'd better get back to it." A gnarled hand rose to stroke the stubbled chin. "That is before you get taken back. I'd hate to whistle up the boys. Why don't you just go along quietly now and maybe lie down for a spell?"

"I can't," said Kevin. "I'm looking for a girl. Have you seen her? Tall, young, with long, blonde hair. Name of Tarvainen. Crystal Tarvainen."

The oldster looked thoughtful. "Well, now, son, that sort of depends. Maybe I have and maybe I haven't. What you want her for, anyway?"

"She's a criminal," said Kevin firmly. "I've got her under arrest for a murder she did back on Earth. I'm taking her back to stand trial."

"A criminal, eh?" Well, what do you know?" The shadowed eyes narrowed. "Arrest, you say? You a police officer, son?"

"I am."

"You got some kind of identification, maybe?"

Kevin slapped his pockets and frowned. "It's back in the ship but you can take my word for it. You've got to help me find that girl. It's your duty," he pointed out. "You can't refuse. As an accredited representative of Earth I call on you to give me your full cooperation."

"Am I denying it, son? What did she do? Exactly, I mean?"

"She took an axe to her husband. Chopped him to pieces and tried to wash them down the disposal unit in their apartment. A maintenance engineer discovered the crime when he went to clear a blockage."

"Is that so?" The agent shook his head. "I don't hold with killing. I don't hold with it at all. If I was you I'd head north to the caravanseri. You might just be lucky."

"North?"

"That way." The old man gestured down the street. "You want I should send a couple of the boys with you? Just in case?"

"No thanks," said Kevin quickly. "I can manage."

"You sure, son? A woman like that could be hard to handle. If she's killed once she could do it again. It'll be no trouble to send along the boys."

"No," said Kevin again. "I'll get her on my own."

* * * *

The road north wound through giant mounds of fungi every step sending up clouds of nose-tingling spores. Sneezing, eyes streaming, coughing and wheezing Kevin pounded along the trail passing little groups of natives which hopped aside squeaking their annoyance. He could have taken a cab, he realised, found some mechanical form of transport, but he had been in too much of a hurry to act sensibly. Now it would take longer to pick up a conveyance than to complete the journey.

A mile from the spaceport he came to a huddle of low buildings set between more of the giant fungi, their surfaces bright with splotches of vermillion and orange, yellow and purple, magenta and sombre brown. Before the buildings stood a cluster of animals, six-legged beasts looking something like ants. On one of them perched a familiar shape.

"Crystal!" Kevin ran harder, cursing the choking spores. "Crystal!"

She turned, looking at him, toying with the goad in her right hand. Her beast lifted its mid-off leg and rasped a claw along its stomach. As Kevin drew level it turned its head, blinked faceted eyes and chomped its jaws with a harsh grinding of chitin.

Kevin yelled and sprang back. "Crystal, you fool! Get off that thing!"

"Worried about me, darling?"

"Of course I'm worried. I—" He broke off as he saw her smile. "All right," he said bitterly. "So I'm ignorant. I've never ridden anything with legs and don't know how they operate. But will you please get down before that thing gets hungry?"

"You are worried," she said, slipping from the beast and hanging the goad on the carved saddle. "And you came after me. I wondered if you would."

"You knew I would," he snapped. "That's why you did it, didn't you? Run off, I mean. Damn it, Crystal, you gave your word."

"Which you didn't believe," she said coldly. "And, just to remind you, I only promised to return to Earth. I didn't say when. If you hang around long enough we might even go back together."

"You bitch!"

"Is that why you followed me? Because I'm such a bitch?"

"No," he admitted. "It was because I—" Irritably he shook his head. "Never mind."

"But I do mind," she insisted. "I want to find out just what makes you work. Was it the money? The bounty you hope to collect from my father? Is that all I represent to you? A fat bonus paid COD Earth?"

Annoyed at her tone he snapped, "You can afford to sneer. You've never known what it is to go without. Wait until you haven't the money to buy your way out of trouble. When you've got to work for it and do things you'd rather leave alone. Then, perhaps, you'll understand. Oh, to hell with it," he said disgustedly. "You're just a spoilt bitch. To you all this is just a big joke."

"Am I laughing?"

"No," he admitted, staring at her. "You're not laughing. At least not that I can see. But why be so awkward? I tricked you on Illagesh and I admit it but what else could I do? And what would it cost you to keep your bargain? Damn it, Crystal! All I want is to take you back home to Earth."

"Maybe that's the trouble," she said ambiguously. "Maybe you don't want enough."

He frowned, trying to gather what she meant, then jerked his head towards the sky at the sound of a distant thunderclap. Incredulously he looked at his watch.

"That was the *Ullalla*," she said calmly. "Ships do wait for anyone, you should know that. Well, there it is."

He glared at her with abrupt understanding. "You meant this to happen," he accused. "You meant it all the time."

"So?" Her smile was triumphant. "One day, darling, you'll learn that I like to get my own way. I'm a girl who just can't be pushed around."

A trick, thought Kevin bleakly. The whole thing had been acted like a play. The disappearance, the beast she had sat on, waiting until he arrived, ready to move off if he appeared too soon. And now the ship was gone and with it his paid passage and the promised bonus. Damn the girl! But he wasn't beaten yet.

"Don't do it," she warned as he stepped towards her. "I know something about self-defence. Touch me and I break both your arms."

"I'm taking you back," he said tightly. "I'm going to tie you in a bundle and sit on you until the first ship arrives heading for Earth. We'll travel freight if we have to but I'm going to take you home. Damn you, woman," he yelled, rushing towards her. "I'll teach you to make a fool out me!"

Blind with anger he lifted both hands to grip her shoulders. Warily she backed and dodged to one side. His rush sent him hard against one of the beasts which reared and spun on its hind legs, front and middle clawing the air. From before the buildings a cluster of natives squeaked their astonishment at the peculiar goings on.

Kevin ignored them as he did the two riders loping down the road from the spaceport. Determinedly he advanced towards the girl.

"Don't," she said. "Kevin, you idiot, don't make me hurt you!"

And then the sky fell down and mashed the top of his head.

* * * *

Earth stank. The air hit him like a smelly fist as he left the port of the spaceship and looked at the sky beneath which he'd been born. It was a dirty grey, clouded with smog, the sun invisible beyond the haze. All around rose the clamour of voices, the endless din of too many people cooped too close. Beyond the high wall the towers of the city reared like a forest of rotting teeth.

Groaning Kevin woke and stared at a cross-hatch of bars. His head felt a mess and gingerly he touched it finding nothing more serious than a bump. Imagination, he thought, relaxing on the cot. Like the dream. Was Earth really as bad as that?

"You awake, son?" The familiar voice of the agent came from beyond the bars. The seamed face parted in a grin as Kevin sat up and nursed his throbbing temples. "Like something to drink? Real coffee, local grown in a hydroponics farm. Did I tell you it was my hobby?"

"Drinking?"

"Gardening. Here." A gnarled hand passed a steaming mug through the bars. "Guess you feel in a bad way, son."

Kevin reached for the coffee and took a tentative sip. "What happened?"

"You got yourself kicked on the head by a grill. The boys I sent after you fetched you back. The girl too," he added thoughtfully. "You two had the locals real upset. I had to tell them it was a courtship dance—no point in letting them know we tend to violence against each other. Like the coffee, son?"

It was the best he'd ever tasted and Kevin said so. The agent grinned. "Name's McKeef," he said. "That's genuine Brazilian, lightly roasted, fresh ground, you're drinking. Want some more?"

Kevin had some more. His head eased a little and he could guess what had happened. McKeef hadn't trusted him to bring in the girl alone. And he'd been right, thought Kevin bitterly. He'd fouled even that simple operation. She must have split her sides when he'd hit the dirt. But, maybe, she wasn't laughing at this moment. Cautiously he said "Do you have the girl?"

"Crystal Tarvainen? Sure."

"In custody, I mean."

"She's where I can get her if I want," said McKeef. "You don't have to worry about the little lady."

"She's dangerous," said Kevin hopefully. "I told you about her. You'll have to help me get her on a ship heading for Earth as soon as you can."

"Well, now," said McKeef thoughtfully. "I'm not too sure about that. In fact I can't be sure that you'll be going anywhere for quite a spell. Did I tell you that I was the law around here? The natives elected me to keep the peace. I'm the judge too. You figure you'd like working in a hydroponics farm son?"

"What's that got to do with it?" Kevin set down the mug and tugged at the bars. They didn't move. "Why am I locked up? I don't need protection."

"Not you, son," said McKeef gently. "But others might. The steward of the *Ullalla* dumped your gear before taking off. I persuaded him that it was the right thing to do. You know, it's a funny thing, but I couldn't find your identification anywhere."

Kevin forced a smile. "Well, is that so important? You know how it is with these things. It probably got lost somewhere."

"Impersonating an officer of the law," said McKeef dreamily. "Making false accusations against a blameless citizen. Attempted abduction. Attempted mayhem. Son, it seems to me that you're in real trouble. I only hope you like humping grit and cleaning tanks. From where I stand you're going to be here for a long, long time."

He meant it, thought Kevin. The nurd had the misty look of a visionary, the gloating expression of a cat faced with an endless supply of cream. If he wasn't going to find himself trapped in a hydroponics farm for life he'd have to do something about it.

"Now wait a minute." Kevin jerked impatiently at the bars. "You've got it all wrong. It wasn't like that at all. Let me out of here and I'll explain."

"Talk away, son," said McKeef. "The bars don't muffle you none. You were saying?"

"It was a misunderstanding. Me telling you that I was an officer, I mean. I had to exaggerate a little in order to gain your cooperation. The truth is the girl is crazy and needs treatment. Her father placed her under my care and I've been looking after her. She got away and I had to get her back before she hurt someone. Can you blame me for getting what help I could? Wouldn't you have done the same in my position?"

McKeef rubbed his chin. "You a medical man, son?"

"I'm the head psychiatrist of the Mercy Mission Hospital, north sector, Earth," said Kevin flatly. "With degrees from Vienna, London, the Zeng-Finn Academy on Beta Ghinn and doctorates from both San Fransisco and Platarch. That's on Zingara," he explained. "I've also studied under the symbiotes of the Klarda system who, as you must know, are the accepted authority on all matters appertaining to hallucination, illusion and degraded appetites. When I tell you that Crystal Tarvainen is dangerous I mean it. At any moment she could grab one of the natives and start using it for salad."

McKeef looked solemn. "That's a bad prospect, son. But aren't you a little young to have all those qualifications??

"I started early. Now let me out of here before it's late!"

Released he ran from the building and out into dazzling sunlight. The girl, so McKeef had told him, was at the Travellers Haven, room 18, and he headed for the hotel. The way passed the spaceport and he slowed at comforting sight of landed vessels. He still had some money and could buy a passage even if only to the next stop. He could be lucky and land on a world suited to his talents. Something like Illagesh, maybe, where he could find a job and settle down. At least he would escape his present mess. The agent had seemingly been persuaded but there had been something in the way he had grinned when unlocking the cell which Kevin hadn't liked. A cat playing with a mouse, he thought. Maybe Crystal had already left and the old coot was having a little senile amusement. Getting ready for the kill, so to speak. Giving him enough rope to truly hang himself.

If he had any sense at all he'd get on the first ship to leave even if he had to ride as freight.

He had no sense. Before he knew it his feet had carried him past the field and into the hotel. The door slammed behind him and a native squeaked as he headed for the stairs. "Really, sir, you must be announced! Whom do you wish to see?"

Kevin ignored the squeak and raced up the stairs and along a passage eyes searching for the number. He found it and slammed open the door. Crystal Tarvainen, neat, lovely, cool in a misty something, hair a shimmering glory, sat at ease before the window and sipped at a tall glass.

"Well, well," she said. "So you made it. Good for you."

"Crystal!" He paused, fighting the sudden pounding of his heart. "I thought you might have left," he said lamely seeing the quizzical lift of her eyebrows. "Caught a ship out while I was in jail."

"And that would have worried you?"

"You know damn well it would!"

"Why?"

Because I love you, he thought with sudden clarity, but he couldn't say that. He'd ruined his chances with this girl from the beginning. To her he was just a money-hungry bounty-hunter intent on forcing her back to where she didn't want to go. To get emotional now would be to arouse her contempt.

"Why?" she said again, her eyes intent and then, as he remained silent, sighed and finished her drink. "Well, darling, it looks as if I've got to do this the hard way. Right, Pop?"

"I reckon so, miss," said a familiar voice. Kevin spun and glared at the prune-face of McKeef. The agent had entered the room without a sound. He shook his head more in sorrow than anger. "Son, for a man who can talk like you can at times you sure seem short of words."

Kevin frowned. "What are you doing here?"

"I asked him to come," said Crystal. "As a judge he an important function. Help yourself to a drink, Pop. He put up a good show?"

"One of the best," said McKeef busying himself with bottle. "It was a real pleasure to listen to him. I guess I haven't had as much fun in years. You want a drink, son?"

Numbly Kevin took the proffered glass. A fix, he thought. The whole thing had been arranged. The girl of course, her and her damned money. And now they were both getting ready for the big laugh. At his expense, naturally.

"You know, son," said McKeef smacking his lips, "for an intelligent man you sure act mighty stupid at times. From where I stand it seems that you don't know anything about women at all."

"What's that got to do with it?"

"A lot," snapped Crystal. "Listen, you stupid nurd. Remember I told you that I was a girl who got what she wanted? Well, I want you. At first I considered you a damned nuisance and I'll admit it. Then you showed me that you were clever, able to adapt when you had to, and I got interested. Then on Illagesh—"

"Where you walked away and left me stranded," he reminded.

"—where I'd fixed it with the factor to take care of you after I'd gone," she corrected, "you really won me over. What you did was clever even if it would never have up in court. And on the shuttle—" She broke off, shaking her head. "I was crazy. It was there all the time and I never guessed it. I've had too many men chasing me for what they could get so I fought against being attracted to you all the way. Testing you, I guess. Had you whined or begged or shown yourself to be weak I'd have dumped you fast. And then, when we stopped here and you came after me, well, that clinched it. You're what I want, Kevin, and I'm going to have you."

Bleakly he said, "Just like that?"

"Sure."

"Like buying a dog in a pet shop? Something which will amuse you for a while? And then what? Throw it back into the discard? No thanks, Crystal. I'm no toy."

"You're a fool," she said impatiently. "How else can I say it? I'm in love with you, Kevin, can't you understand? I love you and I'm going to have you."

She was too confident and in love or not he had his pride. Also he was cautious. This could be the big build-up for the calculated let-down. Her revenge for him having badgered her. The salve for her wounded ego.

Firmly he shook his head. "No."

"No what? I haven't asked you anything yet."

"You're not going to have me," he said. "That's what I mean."

Sweetly she said, "Kevin, darling, I've already got you. Remember that indenture you signed? I've got it and it gives me a lien on your services for the next twenty years. Right, Pop?"

"That's right," said McKeef. "Son, you haven't got a chance. Take an old man's advice and quit struggling. You may even get to like it after a while."

Kevin smiled his triumph. "You've forgotten something, Crystal. I've a quit-claim on that indenture. See?" He lost his smile as he searched his pockets. "It's gone! You stole it," he accused. "You took it when you got me drunk your tent that time."

"When you tried to get me drunk," she corrected, guess I was in love with you even then but didn't know Well, there it is, Kevin, darling. You're all mine for at least twenty years. You ready to perform the ceremony, Pop?"

McKeef finished his drink. "Just as soon as you're ready, miss. Now, son, if you'll just stand here and take the little lady by the hand we'll get started."

"Now wait a minute," said Kevin. "What ceremony? And what's it got to do with that indenture?"

"Clerical work," mused Crystal rising to stand at side. "Well, you can check the household accounts. Speaking and writing? Naturally you'll have to talk to me and the children and you'll be writing your books."

Kevin took a deep breath, feeling himself caught something over which he had no control. Over which he wanted none. Crystal was quite a girl. "And the rest of it?"

"Serving, manipulation and adjustment?" She looked at him with sparkling eyes. "Why, darling, what else is a husband for?"

www.ingramcontent.com/pod-product-compliance
Lightning Source LLC
Chambersburg PA
CBHW020146180626
46810CB00004B/1750